BROKEN VOWS

What Reviewers Say About
MJ Williamz's Work

Shots Fired

"MJ Williamz, in her first romantic thriller, has done an impressive job of building the tension and suspense. Williamz has a firm grasp of keeping the reader guessing and quickly turning the pages to get to the bottom of the mystery. *Shots Fired* clearly shows the author's ability to spin an engaging tale and is sure to be just the beginning of great things to follow as the author matures."
—*Lambda Literary Review*

"Williamz tells her story in the voices of Kyla, Echo, and Detective Pat Silverton. She does a great job with the twists and turns of the story, along with the secondary plot. The police procedure is first rate, as are the scenes between Kyla and Echo, as they try to keep their relationship alive through the stress and mistrust."
—*Just About Write*

Forbidden Passions

"*Forbidden Passions* is 192 pages of bodice ripping antebellum erotica not so gently wrapped in the moistest, muskiest pantalets of lesbian horn dog high jinks ever written. While the book is joyfully and unabashedly smut, the love story is well written and the characters are multi-dimensional. ...*Forbidden Passions* is the very model of modern major erotica, but hidden within the sweet swells and trembling clefts of that erotica is a beautiful May-September romance between two wonderful and memorable characters."—*The Rainbow Reader*

Sheltered Love

"The main pair in this story is astoundingly special, amazingly in sync nearly all the time, and perhaps the hottest twosome on a sexual front I have read to date. …This book has an intensity plus an atypical yet delightful original set of characters that drew me in and made me care for most of them. Tantalizingly tempting!"
—*Rainbow Book Reviews*

Speakeasy

"*Speakeasy* is a bit of a blast from the past. It takes place in Chicago when Prohibition was in full flower and Al Capone was a name to be feared. The really fascinating twist is a small speakeasy operation run by a woman. She was more than incredible. This was such great fun and I most assuredly recommend it. Even the bloody battling that went on fit with the times and certainly spiced things up!"—*Rainbow Book Reviews*

Heartscapes

"The development of the relationship was well told and believable. Now the sex actually means something and M J Williamz certainly knows how to write a good sex scene. Just when you think life has finally become great again for Jesse, Odette has a stroke and can't remember her at all. It is heartbreaking. Odette was a lovely character and I thought she was well developed. She was just the right person at the right time for Jesse. It was an engaging book, a beautiful love story."—*Inked Rainbow Reads*

Visit us at www.boldstrokesbooks.com

By the Author

BROKEN VOWS

by
MJ Williamz

2018

This Trade Paperback Original Is Published By
Bold Strokes Books, Inc.
P.O. Box 249
Valley Falls, NY 12185

First Edition: October 2018

Credits
Editor: Cindy Cresap
Production Design: Susan Ramundo
Cover Design By Sheri (hindsightgraphics@gmail.com)

Acknowledgments

A huge thank you to all the people who helped make this book a reality. Having attended a Catholic school as a child, I've always been fascinated with nuns. I wrote this book in an attempt to show the human side of those mysterious beings.

Thank you to Laydin for your support and encouragement. As well as being the best sounding board and idea sharer a person could ask for. I love you so much. Sarah, Inger, and Karen were the beta readers for *Broken Vows*, and I value their input more than words can say.

To the awesome folks at Bold Strokes Books—Rad, Sandy, Cindy, Ruth, Stacia, Sheri—and everyone else—thank you so much for all you do. You give my voice a home and work tirelessly to make me a better author.

Finally, thank you to you. A huge thanks to all the readers out there who make writing worthwhile.

Dedication

As always, I dedicate this and everything to Laydin

Chapter One

Maggie watched the woman enter the church. She was tall with short graying hair. She came to Mass every Sunday. She sat in the same pew. And Maggie watched her every time. She couldn't explain what it was, but she felt something for the parishioner. It was deep and visceral. She'd never even spoken to her.

Maybe today, she thought, then turned her mind to focus on the priest and the service.

When Mass was over, Maggie went to the coffee and doughnut social time, hoping to get a chance to talk to the woman. But as was the case every Sunday, the woman wasn't there. Maggie tried to give her undivided attention to those in attendance, but the woman was never far from her thoughts. She remembered the woman's strong looking hands as she went up to receive Communion. She sighed.

"Are you okay, Maggie?" Father Bremer asked her.

"I'm fine, Father," she said.

"That was a heavy sigh. Is there anything you'd like to talk about?"

She looked at him. In his sixties, Father Bremer was bald, with gray eyes that could pierce one's soul.

"No, sir. But thank you."

She took a doughnut and enjoyed it as she made her rounds, talking to the people milling about. Soon the event wound down, and she helped the other nuns clean up. When everything was put away, she walked through the warm garden to the convent.

It was a beautiful day on California's Central Coast, and she decided to go into town. She stripped out of her skirt and blouse and looked at herself in the mirror. She was attractive, for a middle-aged nun, she thought. So why didn't the woman from Mass ever make a point of talking to her?

As she thought of the woman, her stomach tightened, and she felt moisture pool between her legs. She moved her hands over her bra and down her stomach. Her flesh was alive and burned where she'd touched it. She watched in the mirror as she slid her hand under the waistband of her underwear. They were cotton briefs, nothing sexy, but she didn't think the woman would mind.

She slid her hand lower until it was between her legs. She thought again of the woman's strong hands and imagined it was her pleasing Maggie. She cupped her hands and easily plunged her fingers inside herself, pressing her palm into her clit. She rocked on her hand as she stood there watching herself. She closed her eyes and focused on the woman. She pretended she was pleasing her. She thought of nothing but the woman and how good she was making her feel.

In no time, Maggie had to lean against the mirror to keep her balance as first one and then another orgasm rocked her body. She played some more and coaxed two more earth-shattering climaxes from herself.

Breathing heavily, she crossed the room and sat on the bed. It was the first time she'd given in to the fantasies, the first time she'd touched herself as she thought of the stranger. And she felt good, more relaxed than she had in a while. But being the good Catholic nun that she was, she was overcome with guilt. She shouldn't be doing that. Masturbation was wrong. But how could it be if it felt so good? She argued with herself. Sins of the flesh were some of the most dangerous sins there were.

Confused and needing to get out of her own head, she washed her hands and dressed in shorts and a T-shirt. She slipped on her Birkenstocks and was out the door. The church was in the middle of downtown, so it was only a few steps until she was in the cool shade of the little shops. There were throngs of people moving lazily up and down the sidewalk. It felt good to be out in it.

She smelled barbecue and realized how hungry she was. She walked into her favorite bar and grill and had to stand in line to get in. No problem for her. She was a fanatical people watcher. And there were plenty of people on the patio for her to watch. When she was finally let in, she took a seat at the bar since it was the first available. She ordered a beer and a tri-tip sandwich and turned to survey the area inside the restaurant. She had only barely turned when she realized who was sitting next to her. It was the woman from church. She felt her insides burn as she looked her over. She should say something, but what?

The woman must have felt her gaze; she turned to look at her.

"You're a nun from the old Mission, aren't you?" she said.

"I am," Maggie said. "I'm Sister Mary Margaret, but my friends call me Maggie."

"Well, hello, Sister. It's nice to meet you. I'm Alex."

"Please, call me Maggie."

Alex offered her hand and Maggie took it. Her shake was firm. Maggie had been right. Her hand was strong indeed and curiously rough. Maggie flushed at the contact.

"It's nice to meet you, too," she managed.

"I barely recognized you in your casual getup," Alex said. "You always look so nice all dressed up at Mass."

Maggie blushed again.

"Thank you?" she said.

"Yes, it was a compliment. You're always dressed so conservatively, though. I would never have imagined you dressed like this."

"This is my off work attire," Maggie said. "I like to be comfortable when I'm out and about."

"Well, you certainly look comfortable."

"So, what do you do, Alex?" Maggie was anxious to keep the conversation going. Now that she was speaking to her, she never wanted her to stop. Her voice was low and resonating. She could listen to her for hours on end, she was sure.

"I work construction."

"What type?"

"I do it all. Foundation to finish."

"Wow," Maggie said. "That sounds like hard work."

"It is, but it's also rewarding. I love starting with a plot of ground and seeing a house there at the end."

"Do you float from crew to crew or do you have one crew you work with all the time?"

"I have a usual crew. I do odd jobs sometimes, but mostly I work with the same crew."

Their food arrived and they kept up a steady conversation while they ate.

"I see you're out of beer," Alex said. "Can I buy you another one?"

"Sure. Thank you."

Alex ordered them each a beer.

"So, how long have you been a nun?" she said.

"About twenty years now."

"Do you like it?"

"I do."

"Hm," Alex said.

"What?"

"I don't know. It just seems if you loved being a nun and all, you wouldn't be sitting in a bar drinking beer."

"I'm human," Maggie said. "I'm allowed to have fun. I can enjoy the simple things in life."

"I didn't think you were allowed to. I thought all your vows made you unable to have fun."

Maggie laughed. She looked into Alex's deep blue eyes and saw a glimmer of impishness there.

"No, way. I never vowed to give up my humanity just to be a nun."

"Well, that's good to hear."

They finished their sandwiches.

"So, remind me again what you did give up," Alex said.

Maggie laughed again.

"I took my vows of chastity, poverty, and obedience."

"Ah," Alex said. "I couldn't do it."

"Not a lot of people could."

"I need my material things, I admit it. I have never been good at being told what to do, and as for chastity?" She laughed. "There's no way in hell, excuse my language."

Maggie laughed nervously. And blushed profusely.

"Sorry," Alex said. "Didn't mean to shock you."

"I've heard that kind of language before." The words themselves didn't shock her. It was more the vehemence with which she swore she couldn't be celibate that had Maggie heating up. All over, actually. The throbbing below her waist was back. Her stomach was in knots. She knew she needed to get away from Alex.

"Well," she said. "It's been nice meeting you finally. I should get going. I suppose I'll see you at Mass, huh?"

"What's the hurry?" Alex said. "Look, I really am sorry if I offended you."

"You didn't."

"Well, why not have another beer with me? You're easy to talk to. I enjoy your company."

Against her better judgment, Maggie agreed to have one more.

"So, are you from here?" Maggie said.

"Born and raised. Even graduated from Cal Poly."

"So, you went to college and decided to work construction?"

"It was an easy way to stay in town," Alex said. "There aren't a lot of jobs around here, and I wasn't really into moving away. What about you? What's your past look like?"

"I grew up in Kansas. I came here to study at Cal Poly, and that's when I got my calling."

"Your calling, huh? How does that work exactly?"

"It's kind of hard to explain. You just know that this is what you're supposed to do. I don't know if it's God's voice calling to you or what. But you just know."

"Hm."

"Do I sound crazy?" Maggie said.

"Not at all. I just wonder why some people get the calling and others don't."

"I don't have an answer for that. It just happened to me. I just knew I needed to be a nun. I never looked back."

"Did you graduate?"

"I did. I have my teaching credential, which is what I do now. I teach."

"That's cool. I guess I never thought much about what you did outside of Mass. Now I know you teach and hang out here."

Maggie laughed. Her life boiled down that simply, huh?

"Well, I don't usually hang out here. I'll stop by for lunch and then leave and walk the streets. I love to people watch," she said.

"Ah, yes. I hear you there. I love to do that myself."

"Well, why don't we finish our beers and go watch some people?" Maggie couldn't believe she'd suggested that. She really should get away from Alex. She was dangerous, and Maggie felt it to her core.

They finished their beers.

"My truck's parked right outside. Why don't we drive over to the park and watch people there?" Alex said.

"That would be great."

They walked out to the truck, and Alex held Maggie's door open for her.

"Thank you," Maggie said. Surely Alex didn't think she'd never gotten in a truck before?

Alex drove them to the park, and they got out and sat on a park bench. They watched people throw Frisbees for their dogs, ride their bikes, and enjoy the beautiful spring day.

"I can't believe how gorgeous it is today," Maggie said.

"We should be swimming at my place. I have a pool. Do you have a suit?"

"I do," Maggie said.

"Do you want to come over for a dip?"

"That would be great."

"Cool. I'll drive you back to the convent so you can get your suit."

They arrived at the convent and Maggie slid out of the truck. "Did you want to come in?" she said.

"Are you sure? I didn't think we common folk were allowed in the convent."

"You're so funny. Come on. It'll only take a minute."

Alex looked decidedly uncomfortable as she followed Maggie down the hall to her room. Maggie grew uncomfortable, too, as she remembered what she'd done just before she'd left. Oh, well. There was no way Alex could know.

"Wow," Alex said as she looked around the tiny room. "Y'all take the vow of poverty seriously, don't you?"

"We do."

"Well, remember when you see my house, I've taken no such vow."

Maggie laughed.

"You act like I've never been inside a house before. It's fine. Don't worry."

They drove off through town, and on the outskirts, Alex pulled up in front of a nice two-story house. She parked in the driveway and got out. She opened Maggie's door so she could get out.

"Sorry," Alex said. "It's not that I don't think you're capable. It's just habit for me."

"You're very chivalrous, Alex. I like that."

She liked a lot of things about Alex. That is what scared her. And yet, she couldn't make herself say no. She never should have gone to the park with her, let alone come to her house. Nonsense, she told herself. She was here to go swimming. There was no harm in that. Ah, but there was. The harm was in what she was feeling. She wanted Alex, and that was against her vows, the vows she tried so hard to keep. It wasn't easy, and chastity had always been a problem for her. But still, Alex might not even be interested, right? Sure, the way she looked deep into Maggie's eyes made Maggie feel something, but she told herself it was all a figment of her imagination.

Alex opened the front door, and Maggie walked into a rustically furnished home. She immediately fell in love with it.

"I love your place," she said.

"Thanks." Alex shifted from foot to foot. "It's home."

"It's really nice."

"I'm glad you like it." She led her down the hall "Now, here's the downstairs guest room. You can change in there."

Maggie closed the door behind her and took off her clothes. She slipped her bathing suit on and looked in the mirror. There was nothing wrong with her body. She was still in good shape. But no matter how she tried to adjust her breasts, she felt like part of them was exposed. She supposed that was the point of a bathing suit, right? But she was self-conscious. More than she'd been in a very long time.

CHAPTER TWO

Maggie grabbed the towel Alex had given her and wrapped it around her waist. She felt less exposed. What was wrong with her? She'd been swimming millions of times. But she knew. She felt self-conscious because she was attracted to Alex. She hoped—but at the same time was terrified—that Alex was attracted to her, too.

She found Alex already out by the pool. She walked out, and Alex turned and looked her up and down. Maggie blushed under her scrutiny.

"Nice suit," Alex said.

What did that mean? She felt so exposed. She wondered if Alex was being sarcastic.

"Thank you?"

"It is. And it fits you. It's conservative enough for a nun. I like it."

Maggie took in Alex wearing board shorts with a tank top with a sports bra under it.

"And your suit fits you. I can't imagine you in a traditional suit," Maggie said.

"No, way. I'm way too butch for that."

Butch. Yes, she was butch. She was a very handsome butch. Her gaze pierced Maggie's and Maggie had to turn away.

"You ready to get wet?" Alex said.

I already am, Maggie thought.

"Yeah. It's warm enough. Let's get in the water," she said.

Alex went down to the deep end and dove in. Maggie walked to the shallow end and walked down the steps. She sat on the second step, so much of her body was in the water. Alex swam over and sat next to her.

"You comfortable here?" she said.

"I am. This water feels so nice."

"Good." She stood and reached for Maggie's hand. "But come on in all the way. It feels amazing."

Maggie allowed herself to be led into the water. When she got to the point that she had to stand on her tiptoes, she released Alex's hand and dunked herself underwater. She came up to see Alex watching her. She felt really good. That water was amazing.

"There," Alex said. "Doesn't that feel good?"

"It really does."

Alex took her hand again. The electricity coursed through Maggie's body.

"Come on," Alex said. "Swim with me."

Maggie pulled her hand free and swam some laps with Alex. It felt good to stretch her limbs and let the tension go. The water, as she cut through it, kept her focused on the task at hand. It took her thoughts away from Alex and her feelings for her. At least for the moment.

Maggie was running out of steam. She swam for the shallow end, and when she pulled up she saw Alex sitting on the steps.

"Join me?" Alex said.

Maggie sat next to her as she tried to catch her breath.

"Feels good, doesn't it? I love to exercise."

"So do I. I don't do it nearly enough. Except for my walks through town."

"Well, I'm glad you came over today. This has been fun."

Maggie felt like she was getting the bum's rush. She wondered why she was getting kicked out so soon.

"I suppose I should get going," she said.

"Why? What's the hurry?"

Maggie was confused. Alex had said it had been fun. Didn't that mean it was over? That Maggie should leave?

"I thought you were ready for me to leave," she said.

"Quite the opposite. What are your rules for dinner? Like, do you have to eat at the convent?"

"Normally, yes, but Sundays we're on our own." Her heart raced. Was Alex going to ask her out?

"Great," Alex said. "I have a couple of steaks we could grill for dinner. Would you like to stay?"

"That would be great." Maggie heaved a sigh of relief. She wasn't ready for her time with Alex to end.

"Excellent. Why don't you go get changed and I'll get the steaks going? Unless you want to swim some more. That would be fine, too."

Alex's gaze ran lazily over Maggie's body. Maggie felt completely exposed. She was slightly uncomfortable. Only slightly. She liked that Alex seemed to like her body. But she thought for modesty's sake she should change back into her clothes.

"I'll go get changed," she said. "I'll be out in a minute."

She came out of the bedroom to the smell of steaks on the grill. Her stomach grumbled. She hadn't realized how hungry she was.

"That smells divine," she said as she joined Alex on the patio.

"Good. How do you like your steak?"

"Medium rare."

"Me, too. Perfect. They'll be done soon."

"Can I help in any way?" Maggie said.

"You just sit down at the table and relax. I'll get a couple of glasses of wine. I threw together a salad while you were changing."

Alex went inside and returned with a bottle of wine and two glasses. She poured a little into Maggie's glass. Maggie sipped it. It was delicious.

"This is really good," she said. "What is it?"

"It's a Malbec. It's my favorite." She handed Maggie the bottle to check out after she'd filled both their glasses.

Maggie admired the bottle, then set it down and sipped her wine as she watched Alex flip the steaks. She was still in her suit and looked so comfortable in her own skin. Maggie wondered what that would be like. To have that kind of confidence in yourself. Not that Maggie lacked self-confidence. It was different. She couldn't put her finger on it, but she was even more drawn to Alex than before.

Dinner was soon served, and the conversation was easy as they ate.

"This is delicious," Maggie said. "Thank you so much for asking me to stay for dinner."

"My pleasure. It's always more fun to have company than to eat alone."

Maggie laughed.

"Why is it I get the feeling you seldom do anything by yourself?"

"Aw, come on. Sunday nights I always eat alone. Then get to bed early so I can get up for work on Monday morning."

"Okay. I'll buy that," Maggie said. "What time does work start for you on Monday mornings?"

"Around six. We like to start early and finish early in the afternoon. It's nice."

"I know what you mean. Our classes end at three. Of course, then comes grading homework, and everything, so I don't usually finish until after six. Just in time for dinner at six thirty at the convent."

"Do they feed you well? At the convent, I mean."

"Oh, yeah. I mean, we don't eat like this, obviously, but the food is usually good. And there's always enough for all of us."

"How many nuns live in the convent?"

"Right now, there are twelve of us. Thirteen if you include the mother superior."

They finished dinner and Maggie helped clear the dishes.

"Don't worry about washing them," Alex said. "I can do that later."

She poured them each another glass of wine. Maggie was feeling mellow from the wine and good food. She was more relaxed than she'd been in a very long time.

Alex led them to the living room where they sat together on a couch. Alex draped an arm around Maggie's shoulder. Maggie fought the urge to stiffen.

"I really like you, Maggie. My feelings are really torn right now."

"How so?"

"If you were any other woman, I would have kissed you by now. But you're a nun. My feelings are all jumbled up."

"I understand what you're saying. I'm a bit jumbled myself."

"So, you do like me." It was a statement, not a question.

"Of course I do. What red-blooded American woman wouldn't?"

"So are you just red-blooded or are you hot-blooded, too?"

"Right now, I'm a little of both."

"Can I kiss you, Maggie? Or will I go to hell?"

"I think I'm the one who needs to worry about that. I'm the one that took the vow."

"Have you ever broken your vow before, Maggie?" Alex said. "Please tell me."

"I have. I have a hard time with that vow."

"Maggie, I want you."

"Kiss me, Alex." She said it without thinking. She spoke from the need burning deep inside her.

Alex pulled her close, and Maggie watched as she moved closer. She saw her lips part, and Maggie closed her eyes just as their lips met. The kiss was soft and tender, but it caused the need inside Maggie to flare. She turned and snaked her arms around Alex's neck. She pulled her tight against her and opened her mouth to invite her in.

Alex's tongue barely met Maggie's and Maggie's heart raced. When she slid it in farther, Maggie thought she'd pass out from the desire that threatened to overwhelm her. She felt herself growing wet, her need for Alex growing with each passing minute.

Alex broke the kiss and rested her forehead against Maggie's. They were both breathless.

"I need you, Maggie. I've got to have you."

"Take me, Alex. I'll gladly give myself to you."

Alex stood and took Maggie's hand. She led her upstairs to the master bedroom. She laid her down on the log four-poster bed and lay on top of her. Her suit was still damp, but Maggie didn't care. She knew she wouldn't be wearing it for long. Soon it would be off and they would lie skin to skin, and Maggie couldn't wait.

Maggie moved under Alex, pressing herself into her. She needed her with every ounce of her being. All thoughts of her vows were gone, swallowed by the intensity of her need. When Alex skimmed her hand over Maggie's body, she shuddered, the feeling almost too much for her.

"We need to get out of these clothes," Alex said. She stood and Maggie joined her. Alex took Maggie's shirt over her head and unhooked her bra. She stood gazing at her, lust showing in her eyes. She took Maggie's breasts in her hands and ran her thumbs over her nipples. Maggie gasped.

"Oh, my God, you feel so good," she said.

"I want to make you feel good, Maggie. I want to make you feel things you've never felt before."

"Please do. I need you. I trust you."

Alex unzipped Maggie's shorts and slipped them off. Maggie shuddered at her touch. She stood in her underwear. What would Alex say if she knew that just hours before Maggie had touched herself thinking of her? She hadn't even known her name then. And now, here she was, standing in just her underwear in front of Alex. In person. She slid her underwear down her thighs, and Alex's eyes darkened. When she stepped out of her cotton briefs and stood naked, Alex gasped.

Maggie undressed Alex slowly and deliberately, enjoying each patch of skin as it was exposed. She kissed her shoulders and down her chest. She bent to take first one nipple and then the other in her mouth. She ran her tongue lovingly over each. Alex groaned and threaded her fingers through Maggie's hair. Maggie smiled to herself.

"Do you like that?"

"Don't ever stop."

When she had Alex naked, Alex pulled her to her again. The feel of Alex's bare skin against hers had moisture pooling between her legs. She was on fire and Alex's skin burned into her, fanning the flame.

Alex kissed her hard. Their tongues danced together, and Maggie was certain she would self-combust any moment. She pressed into Alex with all her might. She wanted to feel every inch of her. Needed to feel all of her.

Maggie finally pulled away and looked into Alex's eyes.

"Take me," she whispered.

Alex eased her on the bed and climbed on top of her. She ground into her as they kissed. Maggie loved the feel of Alex on top of her. She wanted to feel the weight of her forever. Alex moved off her and lay beside her, gazing at her body. She brought her gaze back to Maggie's eyes and looked into them.

"You have the most beautiful green eyes I've ever seen," Alex said.

"Thank you."

Alex skimmed her hand over Maggie's body, never taking her focus off Maggie's eyes. Maggie tried to keep her eyes open, but it was a losing battle. She closed them, lost in the feel of Alex's touch.

When Alex slipped her hand between Maggie's legs, she sucked in a large gasp of air.

"You're so wet and warm," Alex said. "You feel amazing."

She slid her fingers inside Maggie and Maggie cried out at the feeling.

"Oh, my God, you feel so good," she said.

Alex kissed lower on her body. She stopped to suck a nipple, playing with it in her mouth. Maggie groaned.

"You're torturing me."

Alex kissed lower still and nipped at her belly. Maggie squirmed on the bed, urging Alex deeper inside and lower down her body. Alex was finally between Maggie's legs. She licked and sucked at Maggie's clit while she continued to move in and out of her.

Maggie bucked off the bed, lost in the feelings Alex was causing. She met each thrust and gyrated to make sure all her favorite spots were stroked. She pressed Alex's face into her as she felt a giant ball of energy coalesce inside her. She moved up and down and all around, getting closer by the second. Finally, the ball exploded, shooting white heat throughout her body, leaving her limp as a noodle.

Alex didn't stop. When Maggie's grip loosened, she licked down so she could suck her lips. She reveled in the flavor of Maggie's orgasms. She dipped her tongue inside Maggie, licking and thrusting her tongue.

Maggie, not nearly sated by her orgasm, felt the tension coil inside again. She focused on Alex and cried out again as another climax tore through her body.

When Maggie quit shuddering, Alex moved up next to her. She kissed her hard on her mouth, sharing Maggie's flavor with her.

"You taste amazing," she said. "But I knew you would."

"And now it's my turn to taste you," Maggie said.

She slid between Alex's legs.

"You're beautiful."

She licked at Alex's clit and felt her shiver. She moved lower and lapped inside her. She tasted so good. Maggie could have stayed there all night. She licked back to Alex's clit and sucked it between her lips. She ran her tongue along it and felt Alex's hand on the back of her head. Maggie could barely breathe, but she persevered. She sucked and licked and flicked Alex's clit, teasing her until Alex called her name and then went limp on the bed.

Maggie climbed up next to her and settled into her arms.

"Well, I must say," Alex said. "Today ended much differently than I'd ever expected."

"Me, too." Maggie was already starting to feel guilty. She pushed the guilt down deep inside herself. She wanted to at least enjoy the moment. She looked over and saw the clock. "Oh, dear. I need to get going. Curfew is ten o'clock."

They hurriedly got dressed, and Alex drove Maggie back to the convent. There was no time for long good-byes although Maggie did want to ask if she'd see Alex again. But the words didn't come out.

"Thank you for a great day," Alex finally said.

"Thank you."

"Have a good night."

"You, too."

Maggie walked into the convent and ran into her mother superior.

"Where have you been, Maggie?" she said.

Maggie gulped.

"I went swimming and had dinner with a parishioner."

"Oh, good. That makes me proud. That's a good job."

"Thank you, Reverend Mother."

"Good night, Maggie."

"Good night, ma'am."

Chapter Three

The following Sunday, Maggie was on autopilot singing the processional hymn. She kept her focus on the door waiting, hoping, to see Alex. But she didn't show up. Maggie felt a lump in her stomach. She'd been used and dumped. It was reality. She was sure Alex wasn't the settling down type. But she still hoped to see her. She'd missed her as she went through the week. Thoughts of her constantly occupied her mind when it was at rest. She'd looked forward to Sunday like she never had before.

Resigning herself to the fact that Alex wasn't coming, she took a deep breath and turned her focus to the Mass. She prayed hard during the Mass for forgiveness, even as she longed to see Alex again. She was confused.

After Mass, she went to the coffee and doughnut hour as usual. She forced herself to put on a smile as she interacted with the parishioners. Many of her students were there with their parents, so she spent time talking to each of them.

She was back at the table grabbing a doughnut when she heard a voice behind her.

"Am I allowed to have a doughnut even if I missed Mass?"

The voice sent white-hot chills down her spine. She turned to see Alex standing there smiling at her.

"Of course you can." Maggie tried to play cool, but she was shaking all over.

"I overslept. I was out late last night," Alex said.

"Oh. Did you have fun?"

"Yeah. It was okay."

"Good."

They stood in awkward silence.

"Now," Alex said. "About that doughnut?"

Maggie stepped out of her way.

"Oh, yeah. Help yourself."

Alex took a doughnut and stepped back to look at Maggie.

"So, I was wondering," she said. "Would you like to come over and go swimming again today?"

Maggie's heart lurched. She would love to. And she hoped she knew where that would lead.

"That would be great."

"I can hang around until this is over and then you can get your suit and I'll drive you to my place."

"That sounds wonderful. For now, though, I need to mingle. If you'll excuse me?"

"Oh, of course."

It took every ounce of energy Maggie could muster to pull herself away from Alex. She wanted to stand there, lost in her eyes. Her deep blue eyes that conveyed as much longing for her as she felt herself. But she needed to talk to the other parishioners, so she did.

The event wound down, and Alex helped the nuns clean up. She walked with Maggie across the gardens to the convent.

"It's a beautiful day today," she said.

"It really is."

"You kind of need to spend it in a pool, don't you?" Alex said.

"It's the perfect day for that."

They were in the convent then, and Alex stopped talking. She seemed nervous.

"Does the convent make you uncomfortable?" Maggie said.

"It intimidates me. I'll admit it. But I also just feel like I don't belong here. Like someone's going to see me and kick me out."

"You don't need to worry about that. You're with me. You're my guest."

"Okay. I'll try to mellow out."

They arrived at Maggie's room and went inside. Maggie's palms itched. She wanted to reach out and pull Alex to her. She wanted to kiss her, to feel their lips pressed together. But she did no such thing. She kept herself together and grabbed her swimsuit from its drawer.

"I'm ready," she said.

"Do you really kneel there and pray?" Alex motioned to the kneeler situated under a crucifix on the wall.

"I do, why?"

"I don't know. Just wondered."

They walked in silence to Alex's truck. Maggie was wondering if Alex was having second thoughts. She hoped not. She was excited at the prospect of being with her again. She broke the silence when they got in the truck.

"So, what did you do last night that kept you out so late?"

"If you must know, I was at the women's club. I was dancing the night away."

Maggie felt a powerful sense of jealousy wash over her. She told herself to calm down. She didn't own Alex. But she was still disappointed. She wished she hadn't asked. But the next burning question wouldn't stay inside.

"Did you find someone to take home?"

Alex looked at her silently for a moment. Maggie's heart sank. She had no reason to feel this way. She had the feeling Alex was a player. She couldn't expect a woman like her to be true to her.

"No," Alex said quietly. "I didn't take anyone home. To be honest, I can't get you out of my head, and I'm really not used to that."

Maggie's heart soared as they pulled up in front of Alex's house. She didn't say anything as they got out of the truck and went in the house. As soon as Alex closed the door behind her, she took Maggie in her arms.

"Do you understand what I'm saying?" she said.

"I think so. I've thought of little but you this past week as well."

"But don't get used to it," Alex said. "I can't promise to give up my womanizing ways altogether."

"I can't ask you to," Maggie said, though deep inside she wanted her to.

Alex bent her head and claimed Maggie in a deep, soul-searing kiss. Maggie felt her toes curl. When she came up for air, she looked into Alex's eyes and saw the familiar longing. She knew she was in trouble again, but didn't care. She'd deal with the guilt afterward, but first, she'd enjoy the night.

"Come on in," Alex said. She moved away from Maggie but kept hold of her hand. She led her to the guest room. "You want to change into your suit now?"

"Do you want to help me?" The words were out before Maggie realized it.

"I'd love to."

Maggie saw Alex's eyes darken to yet another shade. They were filled with lust, a complete lust that matched Maggie's own.

Alex unbuttoned Maggie's church blouse and dropped it on a chair. She took her bra off next and laid it on top of her blouse. Maggie stood there awaiting her touch. Her breasts needed to feel Alex's hands on them. But Alex left them alone. She unzipped Maggie's skirt and placed it on the pile of clothes. She knelt and removed Maggie's underwear. Alex kept her cheek against Maggie's thigh and breathed deeply.

"You smell like heaven," she said.

Maggie shifted slightly so Alex was between her legs. Alex stood.

"Not yet, my dear," she said. She took off her clothes and pulled Maggie against her.

"I love the feel of our bodies together," Maggie said.

"Mm. Me, too." She kissed Maggie then, another hard, passionate kiss. Maggie found it hard to keep her balance.

"Let's lie down," she said.

They fell onto the bed and tangled their limbs together. Maggie rolled over on top of Alex. Alex bent her knee, and Maggie ground herself into it. She moved up and down, leaving a trail of wetness on Alex's leg. She ground harder when Alex took one of her nipples in her mouth.

Maggie cried out as the orgasms cascaded over her.

"I need to taste you," Alex said. She rolled over and kissed down Maggie's body until she was between her legs. She lapped up all evidence of her orgasm and all the new juices that flowed there. She buried her tongue as deep as it would go. Maggie moved against her face, urging her onward.

Alex slid her fingers inside Maggie and sucked her clit. Maggie called her name as she climaxed again and again.

"You're so easy," Alex said.

"Is that a bad thing?"

"Not at all. It's nice."

"Oh, then, thanks."

"You're welcome."

"My turn now," Maggie said. She kissed Alex and tasted her own flavor on her lips. She did taste good. Alex was right. Maggie skimmed her hand all over Alex's tight body. She stopped to knead a breast and tweak a nipple that was already rock hard. She pinched it and twisted it until Alex was breathing heavily.

She moved her hand lower to where Alex's legs met. Alex spread herself and arched her hips to beg Maggie not to stop. Maggie had no intention of stopping. She delved her fingers deep inside Alex and stroked her satin walls. Alex moved under her, up and down, meeting each thrust. Maggie pressed her thumb into Alex's clit, and Alex screamed her name as she came.

They lay together for a few minutes.

"That was nice," Alex said. "Thank you."

"Oh, no. Thank *you*."

"You ready to swim now?"

"I am."

"Okay. You put your suit on, and I'll go get mine on. I'll meet you out back."

Maggie got to the pool first. She walked down the steps and sat on the second step, enjoying the feel of the water on her.

"You look at home here," Alex said as she stepped in to join her.

"I don't know if that's a good thing or not."

"Neither do I."

"What are we doing?" Maggie said. She didn't want the answer but had to ask.

"I don't know. I told you. I'm not the one-woman type."

"I get that. And I can't ask you to be."

"No," Alex said. "You're not exactly in the position to ask that of me."

"No. I'm not."

"I say we just enjoy whatever it is we have and not ask too many questions or delve in too deep, okay?"

"That sounds great," Maggie said.

Alex kissed her then. It was a gentle kiss that still sent Maggie's hormones surging. What was her problem? She should have been completely satiated by that point. And yet she wanted more, needed more. She kissed Alex back and tried to keep it soft.

"Come on," Alex said. "Let's swim."

They swam some laps, and when Maggie was tired, she sat on the step and watched Alex. Alex finally stopped and came over to join Maggie.

"That felt so good," she said. "I love to swim."

"So do I. Thank you for inviting me over."

"Clearly, I invited you for more than just a swim."

Maggie blushed.

"Clearly."

"Are you ready for an early dinner?" Alex said. "We didn't have lunch, and I'm getting hungry."

"Dinner sounds good. My stomach is growling, and I hadn't even thought about food."

"I have some salmon I can grill. Does that sound good?"

"Sounds great," Maggie said. "I love a good salmon."

"Good. Should we get dressed or stay in our suits?"

"Let's stay in our suits," Maggie said. "We can change later."

"Yeah. After dinner. I look forward to taking your suit off slowly and deliberately."

Maggie blushed a deep crimson. She felt the heat start at her chest and work its way up. She had no way to hide it.

"You're cute when you blush," Alex said.

"Thanks. I guess."

"You are. You'll have to trust me."

She kissed Maggie, and it turned into a deeper kiss than Maggie had anticipated. She wrapped her arms around Alex's neck and pulled her close. The kiss went on forever, and when they finally came up for air, Maggie couldn't speak.

"No more kisses like that until after dinner," Alex said. "Otherwise we'll never eat."

"Yes, ma'am." Maggie smiled.

Alex got out of the pool and dried off.

"Do you need some help?" Maggie said.

"Nope. I've got it. You just stay where you are. Or you can get out. It's up to you."

When Alex went in to get the salmon, Maggie got out and dried off. She sat in a patio chair and relaxed in the sun. Alex came out and started the barbecue. She put the salmon on and turned to look at Maggie.

"You comfortable?" she said.

"Very. Is that okay?"

"Scary, but okay."

"I don't mean to complicate your life," Maggie said.

"I can't promise that you will. Sure, I couldn't get my mojo on last night because I couldn't get you out of my head, but I can't promise that's going to happen the next time I go out."

"I get that. I really do." The words hurt Maggie deep inside, but if she was honest with herself, she couldn't ask Alex to be faithful to her.

"But for now, it's okay. I'm glad you're comfortable here."

"Great."

"There's a bottle of white wine in the fridge," Alex said. "You mind bringing it out with the glasses I set on the counter?"

"Sure."

Maggie walked into the house feeling quite at home. It was strange, but she liked it. She found the wine and the glasses and walked back outside. She poured them each a glass and took Alex's glass to her just as she was taking the salmon off.

"Thanks," Alex said. "Dinner's ready. I'll go get the salad I made earlier. Sit. We'll eat in just a minute."

Maggie sat down and sipped her wine. The coolness felt good going down. The day was hot, and her hormones had her overheating even more. Alex served their dinner, and they ate with pleasant conversation.

"How was your week?" Alex said.

"It was good. The usual. But the kids were good. Nice and attentive, so it was a winner week. How was yours?"

"Mine was great. We're building apartments over off Broad Street. It's a project that will keep us busy for a while. I'm happy about that."

"That's wonderful."

When they finished, they again cleared the table together and set the dishes in the sink.

"Let's go upstairs," Alex said. "I need you again."

"Lead the way."

They stepped into Alex's room, and Alex stripped Maggie's suit off her. Standing there nude in front of Alex made Maggie want her all the more. She wanted her to take her and have her way with her again.

Alex undressed and took Maggie to the bed. She lay on top of her and kissed her. She ground her hips into Maggie. Maggie wrapped her legs around her, pulling her closer, as close as she could get. She felt Alex's breasts pressed into her and lost herself in the feelings that threatened to overwhelm her.

Alex moved so she lay next to Maggie and placed her hand between her legs. She slowly dragged her hand over every inch of her before entering her.

"More," Maggie said. "I need more."

Alex slid another finger inside, and Maggie groaned.

"You feel so good," Maggie said.

"So do you."

Alex slid her fingers out and rubbed Maggie's clit. She rubbed it hard and fast and Maggie grit her teeth before she cried out. She called Alex's name over and over as the orgasms washed over her.

Maggie lay there catching her breath. When she had recovered, she slipped her hand between Alex's legs. She stroked deep inside her and touched all her soft spots. She pulled her hand out and played over Alex's slick clit.

Alex put her hand on top of Maggie's, and together they rubbed her clit until she came.

They lay together quietly, Maggie lost in her thoughts of what she had just done and what she hoped to do again.

"You okay?" Alex said.

"I'm great. You?"

"Oh, yeah."

"Good."

"Do I need to get you home?" Alex said.

"Yeah. You really should."

"Okay. Go ahead and get dressed and I'll meet you downstairs."

The drive back to the convent was quiet, but Alex held Maggie's hand the whole way.

"You sure you're going to be okay?" Alex said as Maggie got out of the truck.

"Yeah. I'm fine. I'm a big girl, Alex. Will I see you at Mass?"

"Plan on it."

"Okay. See you then."

She let herself into her room and fell onto her bed, her thoughts jumbled.

Chapter Four

Monday morning, even before she went down the hall to take her shower, Maggie dropped onto the kneeler and bowed her head to pray. She prayed for God's guidance in the matter of Alex and begged His forgiveness for her sins. She even reached back to when she was a kid and said the Act of Contrition. She said the last line out loud.

"I firmly resolve, with the help of Thy grace to sin no more and to avoid the near occasions of sin. Amen."

She knelt there thinking about what she had just prayed. She had promised God she wouldn't sin again. Surely God knew that wasn't possible for a mortal. And she had also said she'd avoid the near occasions of sin. Had she just promised God she'd avoid Alex altogether? Was she strong enough to do that?

She took her shower and got ready for her day. She went to the school and prepped for the school day.

Classes went well that day. She had the best students. She had to admit that. They were smart and willing to learn. That day she'd done a little science lesson about static cling. The kids were all attentive, and when she told them to start their homework, the room was silent.

As the kids worked, Maggie was allowed to sit and think. And, hard as she tried to prevent it, her thoughts inevitably kept turning to Alex. Alex at church. Alex in the pool. Alex lying on top of her. She shuddered and brought herself back to the present.

She needed to think long and hard about Alex. She was darned near obsessed with a woman who was a self-proclaimed player. She was only going to break Maggie's heart. But Maggie's heart shouldn't be available to be broken. It should belong only to God.

The bell rang and shook her from her reverie. She stood at her desk and accepted the homework that many of the kids had finished in class.

"Remember, if you didn't finish today, it's due tomorrow," she said as the kids filed out.

She gathered up the homework and slid it in her briefcase. She left the classroom and went to the office to check her mailbox. Yes, they still had mailboxes. It was how messages were still passed on to the nuns. Her parish didn't have computers for the nuns. They were considered unnecessary material objects. The same thing went for cell phones. Nuns were forbidden to have them. They had several phones in the convent that could be used, but they were all in public places. No nun had a phone in her room. Except for Mother Superior.

As she approached her mailbox, it looked empty, but then she saw a small piece of pink paper. It was a phone message. Alex Foster had called and was requesting a callback. Her phone number was written there. Maggie started to shake. Alex had called her. Her heart was in her throat. What to do? It would be rude not to call her back. She walked back to the convent with her emotions battling. She felt excited and guilty at the same time. She needed to make some decisions about Alex. And soon.

Her stomach fluttered and her heart raced as she dialed the number on the slip of paper.

"Hello?" the familiar voice said.

"Alex?"

"Yes. Is this Maggie?"

"It is. You called?"

"I did. I know you said you normally eat dinners at the convent, but can you get a, I don't know, dispensation for tonight? I'm in the mood for Italian, and I don't want to go by myself."

"I don't know, Alex."

"Come on, Maggie. It's just dinner."

"Okay. I'll ask my mother superior if I may be excused from dinner tonight. I'll call you back."

"Okay. That sounds great. I'll talk to you soon."

Maggie was confused when she hung up the phone. She knew better than to go out with Alex, but she wanted to. She needed to. She craved her regardless of how wrong she knew it was to do. She walked into Mother Superior's office.

Mother Superior looked up from her paperwork.

"Hello, Maggie. How may I help you?"

"Reverend Mother, I've been invited to dinner tonight by a parishioner. I was wondering if I could be excused from dinner tonight?"

"Of course, Maggie. I like how involved you are getting into the lives of parishioners. I'm very proud of you."

"Thank you, Reverend Mother."

Feeling even guiltier, Maggie went back to a phone and called Alex.

"I'm free for dinner," Maggie said quietly.

"Are you okay?"

"Yes. Or I will be. Don't worry about me. Please."

"I can't help it. I know I'm messing up your life, but I can't stay away."

"We can talk about it over dinner," Maggie said. "Where are we going, by the way?"

"Mama Italiano's. I love their food."

"Sounds good to me. And it's casual. That sounds good to me."

"Yep. Shorts and T-shirts fit in fine there."

"Okay, well, what time will you pick me up?" Maggie said.

"I'll pick you up at six."

"Great. I'll see you then."

Maggie went to her room and changed into shorts and a T-shirt. She sat at her desk and forced herself to focus on grading the homework from the day. She worked diligently, and when she looked up from it, it was already five thirty. She took a deep breath and wondered what to do to get rid of the amped up feeling coursing through her body. She opted for a nice quiet walk through the gardens.

The gardens were in full bloom, and she stopped to smell all the flowers. The roses smelled amazing, but it was the irises that she truly loved. She stared at the rows and rows of them and felt the calming power they always had over her. She was lost in them when she heard the sound of a vehicle. She looked up to see Alex's truck in the parking lot.

Maggie walked to the truck on shaky legs, her excitement to see Alex undeniable.

Alex got out of her truck and walked over to meet her. She pulled her into a tight embrace that lasted a bit too long.

"I hope no one saw that," Maggie said.

"What? You're not allowed to be hugged? I think you deserve to be hugged."

"Thanks, but you know what I mean."

"I think you're being paranoid," Alex said. "But if it makes you uncomfortable, I won't hug you here again."

"Thanks."

They got in the truck, and Alex fired it up.

"How was your day?" she said.

"It was great. We had a lot of fun in school today. How was your day?"

"Brutal. It's gotten so hot, and we were pouring concrete this morning. We had to work to get it down and right before it started to dry. Not an easy feat."

"I'm sorry."

"That's okay. We did it, and it turned out great."

"Oh, I'm happy to hear that."

Alex took Maggie's hand. Maggie stiffened.

"Are you nervous, Maggie?" Alex said.

"A little. Okay. A lot."

"Why? It's just me."

"You're dangerous. I know you are. And yet I'm drawn to you like a moth to a flame."

Alex laughed.

"Dangerous? Me? I hardly think so."

"Yes, you are. And you know it."

"I'm just a woman, Maggie. A confused woman who really likes you and doesn't understand it."

"I don't understand it, either. You could have your pick of women. And, clearly, you do. Why me, Alex? I don't get it."

They tabled their conversation once they were inside the restaurant and waiting to be seated. Once shown to a table, they each picked up their menu and perused it. Maggie took longer than necessary to look at hers. She'd known what she wanted since she'd heard Italian food earlier in the day. But she couldn't put her menu down. Couldn't make herself look at Alex. She knew once she did, she'd be lost in those blue eyes and would lose any resolve that was left. And there wasn't much.

Alex finally reached over and took her menu from her.

"Are you avoiding me?"

Maggie didn't answer, but felt the blush start at her neck and work its way up to her scalp.

"Ah, the telltale blush," Alex said.

"I'm sorry. I'm so darned nervous."

"What can I do to alleviate that?"

"I don't know."

"Neither do I."

They ordered and then sat there quietly for a bit.

"What are you doing to me, Maggie?"

"I don't know. And why me? I don't understand."

"I can't stop thinking about you. I almost fucked up today, excuse my language. I almost messed up today because I was spacing out thinking of you. I can't get enough of you. That's not my style, Maggie. I usually take a woman home, have my fun and forget about her the next day. I've been that way for years. I like being that way. I never wanted to change. But now, I can't even pick up another woman. All I want is you."

"Oh, Alex. But it's so complicated. I'm a nun."

"Believe me. That fact is never far from the forefront of my mind."

"Mine, either."

Maggie wondered whether she should tell Alex about her prayer session that morning. She opted against it. She couldn't figure out why, but she didn't think it would be a good idea.

"Penny for your thoughts? You looked pretty lost in them there for a minute."

"No. Not worth a penny."

"Okay. Suit yourself."

Their meals were served, and they ate in relative silence with only a smattering of conversation. When their dishes had been cleared, Alex cleared her throat.

"So, I guess asking you back to my place for a nightcap is a bad idea?"

"Oh, Alex. You know I can't say no to you. That's part of the problem."

"I won't apologize. Come on, let's go."

They drove in silence to Alex's house. Once inside, Alex kissed Maggie. It was soft, tentative. Maggie opened her mouth and invited Alex in. The kiss deepened, and Maggie's resolve weakened proportionately. She was weak in the knees when the kiss finally ended, and she held on to Alex for support.

"That was nice," Alex said. She was breathing heavily, and Maggie knew she wanted her as much as Maggie wanted Alex.

Alex took Maggie's hand and led her to the couch. Maggie stood there looking down at it. It was safe. Safer than the bedroom, but Maggie didn't want safe. She was past that.

"Wouldn't the bedroom be more comfortable?" she said.

Alex looked deeply into her eyes.

"Are you sure about that?"

Maggie nodded, words escaping her.

Alex took her to the downstairs guest bedroom. Maggie was happy. It was closer, and the sooner she could have Alex, the better. Alex pulled her close and kissed her again. Maggie pulled back and took Alex's shirt off. They fumbled together to get her shirt over her head, and then they broke apart and each finished undressing on her own.

They lay on the bed with Alex on top of Maggie. She brushed a piece of hair off her face.

"I love your hair," Alex said. "It's soft and silky. And I like that you don't color it. The blond with the gray streaks looks stunning."

"Thank you," Maggie said. She looked up at Alex as she spoke and felt her heart soar. Alex was so gorgeous, and it made her happy to think that Alex found her attractive as well. Of course she did or she wouldn't be with her, Maggie knew, but still, it was nice to hear.

Alex kissed Maggie again and rubbed their bodies together. Maggie's need grew with each passing moment.

"I need you, Alex. Take me."

Alex moved down Maggie's body until she was between her legs. She inhaled the scent that was all Maggie and her mouth watered. She lowered her mouth to take Maggie's slick clit in her mouth. She played over it with her tongue. Maggie squirmed on the bed. Alex slid her fingers inside her and Maggie arched to take her in. She moved all around on the bed, urging Alex deeper. She placed her hand on the back of Alex's head and held her in place as she felt the energy building up at her center. She closed her eyes. Nothing in the world mattered but the sensations Alex was creating. She felt the energy burst forth and cascade over her body as one orgasm after another washed over her.

When her body had quit shuddering, she opened her eyes to find Alex looking into them.

"Hey," Alex said.

"Hey. That was amazing."

"Thanks. I love pleasing you."

"And now it's my turn to please you," Maggie said.

Alex lay on her back and spread her legs.

"Help yourself," she said.

Maggie kissed her hard on the mouth before kissing down her cheek to her ear. She sucked on an earlobe and heard Alex's sharp intake of breath. She grinned and nibbled her neck.

"Oh, God, the way you make me feel," Alex said.

Maggie kept kissing lower until she came to a small breast. She licked the nipple and watched it respond. She took it in her mouth and pressed the hardened tip against the roof of her mouth as she played over it with her tongue.

She skimmed her hand down Alex's taut belly until she came to where her legs met. She slid her hand lower and felt the wet heat between her legs. She slipped her fingers inside and felt as deep as she could get. She loved how soft and tight Alex was. She moved her fingers in and out, and Alex arched to meet each thrust. Maggie slid her fingers out and pressed them into Alex's slick, hard clit. She rubbed it hard and fast, and Alex called her name as she climaxed.

Maggie moved up into Alex's arms. They were strong and felt so good wrapped around her. She rested for a few moments before she looked over at the clock.

"I should get going," she said.

"Do you have to? Can't you spend the night? Just once?" Alex laughed. It was good to hear the laughter, so Maggie knew she wasn't serious. Otherwise, it might have been tempting.

They rode back to the convent holding hands.

"I'm really into you, Maggie. And I know I'm complicating your life, like I said. So, what should I do? What do you want me to do?"

"I don't know, Alex. It's like I'm addicted to you. And I don't want to give you up."

They arrived at the convent.

"When can I see you again?" Alex said.

"Let's see if we can make it until Sunday. We'll plan on another swim date then."

"Okay. I'll try to leave you alone until then. But know, even if you don't hear from me, that I'm thinking about you."

"Thank you. I'll be thinking of you, too."

Maggie got out of the truck and cut through the garden. She entered the convent and made her way to her room. She stood there, staring at the kneeler under the crucifix. She knew she should kneel and pray for forgiveness. But how could something that felt so right be wrong?

She undressed and climbed into bed, but sleep escaped her. Her mind was full of jumbled thoughts, arguments pro and con over seeing Alex again. But it didn't matter. She'd already agreed to see her next Sunday. And Maggie couldn't wait.

Chapter Five

The rest of the week dragged by for Maggie. She couldn't wait until Sunday. She couldn't wait to see Alex again. But the more her excitement grew, the more her guilt grew. She spent hours praying for guidance, for an answer from God. But God didn't seem to be listening. Unless he was telling her to continue seeing Alex, because that's all she could think about.

Sunday finally got there. Once again, Maggie was on autopilot singing the processional hymn. She stared at the door to the church, willing Alex to walk in. She finally saw her, and her heart skipped a beat. She watched her make the sign of the cross with the holy water and find her usual pew. She watched her long, lithe body genuflect before entering the pew.

Please look at me, Maggie thought. She needed to make eye contact with her.

But Alex stood there watching the processional and singing. Maggie chastised herself for her selfish thoughts. Alex was here for Mass, not for her. She'd see her after Mass, and they'd have a wonderful time.

Maggie started the next verse of the song before she realized the rest of the church was silent. She blushed, feeling the gaze of every parishioner on her. Including Alex, who smiled at her.

Maggie put her hymnal down and focused on the Mass. When it was over, she went to the coffee and doughnut social as usual.

"You have a wonderful voice," Alex said as she grabbed a doughnut. Maggie blushed three shades of red.

"I can't believe I did that."

"You were into the music. I think that's great."

"I think I was preoccupied. And I'm not supposed to be preoccupied in Mass."

"I'm sure God will forgive you."

"Are you sure about that? Because I seem to be asking myself that question more and more lately."

"I'm sorry, Maggie."

"No. I am. You don't need to hear that."

"Sure I do. It involves me, doesn't it?"

"Yes, it does."

"So I need to hear it," Alex said.

"Okay. I get that."

"Good. So, I suppose you need to mingle?"

"I do."

"Go for it. I'll be here."

"Maybe you could socialize, too," Maggie said.

"We'll see. I'm not that active in the parish."

"But you go to Mass every Sunday. It wouldn't hurt you to get to know other parishioners."

"Maybe."

Maggie laughed.

"No promise, huh?" she said.

"No promise."

Maggie made her rounds, stopping to talk to her students and their families. She got called over by the mother superior.

"Yes, ma'am?" Maggie said.

"Hi. I wanted you to meet a new family to our parish. These are the Logans. Their son, Patrick, will be in your class."

"It's wonderful to meet you all," Maggie said. "Will you be starting tomorrow?"

"Yes," Patrick said.

"Well, I look forward to having you in class. What's your favorite subject?"

"I like science."

"We do a lot of that in my class. I love science, too."

They stood awkwardly for a few moments.

"Thank you for coming over, Maggie," Mother Superior said. "I just really wanted you to meet them."

"It's a pleasure." Maggie flashed them a warm smile before turning back to the rest of the congregation.

The social wound down and, as before, Alex helped the nuns clean up. Then, she walked with Maggie to the convent. They ran into Mother Superior as they entered.

"Reverend Mother, do you know Alex Foster?" Maggie said.

"I've seen you at Mass for years now, but don't think we've ever met. It's nice to meet you finally."

"It's very nice to meet you, too, Mother Superior."

"What are you two up to this afternoon?"

"We're going to get a bite to eat then head over to my place to go swimming."

"Oh, how lucky that you have a pool. It's the perfect way to beat this heat. Enjoy yourselves."

She walked off, and Maggie and Alex made their way down the hall to Maggie's room. When the door closed, Alex whispered to Maggie.

"I want to kiss you so bad right now."

"Sh. These walls are paper-thin. Hold your horses for a while. Where are we going for lunch?"

"I don't know. What are you in the mood for?"

Maggie looked Alex up and down and blushed.

"You're so bad," Alex said.

"I can't help it." Maggie grabbed her suit and was ready to go.

"Aren't you going to change?" Alex said. "You look so stuffy in that outfit. It's warm out there. You'll be more comfortable in shorts and a T-shirt."

"With you in here?"

"Now you're getting a sense of modesty?"

"You're right. I'm sorry. I'll change."

Maggie was aware of Alex's close scrutiny as she stripped out of her skirt and blouse and put on her shorts and shirt.

"Okay. Now I'm ready," Maggie said.

"Great. You look much more comfortable. Now, where do you want to go to lunch?"

"How about Firestone's again?"

"Sure, since that's where we first met, it sounds good to me."

As soon as they were in the truck, Alex took Maggie's hand. Maggie loved the feel of her strong, rough hand holding her own. She felt a sense of security, even as her hormones shifted into overdrive.

They arrived at the Firestone Grill and sat on the patio. It was hot, but Maggie loved the heat and the sun felt good. They ate their lunch and sipped their beers.

"I don't know about you," Alex said, "but a swim is going to feel amazing after sitting here in the sun."

"I'm sorry," Maggie said. "You work in the sun all week. You probably would have rather sat inside. I work inside all week, so I welcome the sun and the fresh air."

"It's all good. You wanted to sit on the patio, so here we sit. And don't worry. I love the sun, too."

After Alex had paid the check, they drove to Alex's house. It was familiar to Maggie by then. It felt right to be there. She loved the smell of the place, the feel of it. It was all Alex.

As usual, as soon as the door was closed behind them and they had complete privacy, Alex took Maggie in her arms.

"I think I'm getting used to this," she said.

"Me, too."

Alex lowered her mouth and claimed Maggie's in a heart-stopping kiss. Maggie kissed her back with all the pent up longing she had. Her desire to have Alex and for Alex to have her was complete. She needed nothing else at that moment.

"Whoa," Alex said as she broke the kiss. "That was something else. But if we don't stop now, we'll never make it to the pool."

"Okay," Maggie said. "I'll behave. I'll go put on my suit."

"Maybe today we should swim without suits," Alex said.

"Are you serious?" Maggie blushed profusely.

"Sure. We're far enough from the neighbors on either side. No one can see in my yard. Let's skinny-dip. What the hell?"

"Why not?" Maggie said. She trusted Alex. If she said no one would see them, then what harm was there in it?

"So come here and let me get those clothes off you."

Maggie moved back into Alex's arms. They kissed for a while before Alex pulled away so she could take Maggie's clothes off. When Maggie stood naked, Alex stripped out of her clothes and took Maggie's hand. She led her through the house and out to the pool.

"Have you ever skinny-dipped before?" Alex said.

"No."

"Well, you're going to love it. Come on."

Alex went to the deep end as usual, and Maggie once again went to the shallow end. She stepped into the pool and sat on her usual step. Alex was right. There was something wonderful about being naked in the pool. The water caressed her like an erotic lover. It felt great and did little to quell her overactive hormones.

Alex swam over to her and joined her on the step.

"Feels amazing, doesn't it?" she said.

"It really does."

Alex slid her hand between Maggie's legs.

"Plus it allows for easy access."

Maggie looked at Alex with a pleading in her eyes. She needed her and didn't want to be teased. She turned slightly so her opening faced Alex.

"Oh, I like that," Alex said. She moved her hand down and entered Maggie. Maggie closed her eyes at the feeling. The water moved against her clit as Alex moved inside her. The experience was almost too much. She came instantly and buried her face in Alex's shoulder to keep from crying out.

"Come on," Alex said. "Let's swim."

Maggie swam her usual laps, loving the feeling of the water playing over her naked body as she moved. She quit before Alex did and took her place on the step again. Alex finished swimming and came back to sit next to her.

"You ready to sit in the sun and have a beer?" Alex said.

"Like this?" Maggie motioned to her naked body.

"Sure. I like what I'm seeing. And again, no one can see in my yard."

"Okay, if you're sure."

"I'm positive."

Maggie climbed the stairs, aware of Alex's gaze burning into her. She lay on a lounge chair and willed herself to relax. But she couldn't. Being on display for Alex turned her on as much as seeing Alex in all her glory.

Alex went inside to get the beers. She came out and reached one out to Maggie. When Maggie moved to take it, Alex pulled it away. She placed the cold beverage against one of Maggie's nipples.

"Ouch," Maggie said.

"Did it really hurt?"

"In a good way."

"Good. I almost pressed it between your legs, but that would have heated up the beer."

"You're horrible," Maggie said.

"Thank you."

They lay in the sun and drank their beers.

"What a beautiful day," Maggie said.

"It is. And the company is wonderful. And beautiful."

"Aw. Thank you."

"You're welcome. It's true."

"Well, I happen to find the company charming and handsome."

"Ah. I appreciate that," Alex said.

"Handsome suits you."

"I prefer that term."

"I'll remember that."

"Would you like another beer?" Alex said.

"I think I'd rather take this party inside."

"Oh, yeah? I can do that."

Alex stood and reached out a hand to Maggie. Maggie took it and stood pressed into Alex. They kissed as they stood flesh to flesh, and Maggie was certain the heat would swallow them whole. She was on fire with need and desire. She had to have Alex and soon.

Maggie ran her hands all over Alex's muscular body, from her shoulders down her back to cup her small but firm ass.

"You're making me crazy," Alex said.

"Good. Let's get inside. I'm ready for you."

Alex took her hand and led her upstairs to the master bedroom. Maggie lay on the bed and played with her nipples, and Alex stood watching her.

"Do you ever masturbate, Maggie?"

Maggie blushed.

"Yes."

"Will you masturbate for me? I want to watch you please yourself for me."

Maggie was confused but horny. If that's what Alex wanted, then that's what she would do. She continued to play with her nipples, getting wetter with each passing moment.

"You have such perfect breasts," Alex said. "I don't blame you for spending so much time on them. Tell me what you're feeling."

"I feel good. I feel so good. I can feel myself swelling between my legs. I can feel myself getting wetter by the minute."

Alex licked her lips.

"Good. Make yourself feel good, Maggie. I want to watch you take yourself to new heights."

Maggie moved her hand down her body. She left her left hand on her nipple but slid her right hand between her legs. She was wet and ready for action, even if she had to provide the action herself. She slipped her fingers inside herself and stroked at all her favorite spots. She was losing the battle. She was closing in on her orgasm. She moved her fingers to her clit and rubbed it. She looked at Alex, who had her hand between her own legs.

Maggie closed her eyes and let the orgasm wash over her. She closed her legs around her hand and rode it to the finish.

Alex came at the same time. She called Maggie's name as she did. She climbed on the bed and buried her face between Maggie's legs.

"Your orgasms taste so good," she said. She licked the length of Maggie before dipping her tongue deep inside her, as deep as she could get. She lapped at her walls then moved back to her clit. She sucked it between her lips and flicked her tongue over it. Maggie pressed Alex into her and writhed against her. She arched her hips off the bed, cried out, then collapsed as the climax tore through her.

But Alex wasn't through. She sucked harder on Maggie's clit and slid her fingers inside her. She stroked her slowly at first and then faster as Maggie bucked against her. Maggie screamed as another orgasm claimed her body.

Alex kissed up Maggie's body and lay next to her.

"Oh, my God, what you do to me," Maggie said.

"I love doing that. You know that."

"I know."

Maggie kissed Alex's mouth before she moved lower on her body until she was positioned between her legs. She spread Alex wide and bent to take her in her mouth. She sucked her lips and ran her tongue between them. She moved her tongue to her opening and licked as deep as she could. Her tongue hurt from the exertion, but Alex tasted so good and she needed more of her. She ran her tongue over the rest of her and settled on her clit. She licked it hard and fast until Alex cried out.

They lay together afterward, happy and satisfied. Maggie had never felt that sense of contentment. Not since she'd taken her vows. She shuddered to think of her vows.

"You okay? Are you cold?" Alex said.

"I'm okay. Really. I'm fine."

"You sure?"

"Yeah. But I should probably get going."

"It's still early. You sure you won't stay for dinner?"

Maggie fought an internal struggle. Her vows. Her vow of chastity. Her promise to be faithful to God. She was feeling the guilt already. But more time with Alex? How could she say no? And she was hungry and would have to find something to eat on her own. Why not enjoy dinner with Alex?

"Maggie?" Alex was saying. "Are you okay?"

"I am," Maggie lied. "I'm fine. Sure I'll stay for dinner."

"Great." She was silent for a minute. "Hey, you know, if something we do ever bothers you, you need to talk to me about it, okay?"

Maggie nodded, not trusting her voice. Alex turned Maggie's head so she faced her.

"I mean it. What's bugging you?"

"Nothing. Really. Sometimes I get lost in my head. And think too much. I shouldn't do that."

"Do you feel guilty about us?" Alex said.

"Yes. No. I mean, I do, but never for long. Sometimes it hits me and I wonder what I'm doing, but like I've said, I can't get enough of you. I mean that."

"Okay, well if you need or want to talk about it more, I'm here. I hate to make you feel bad. I only want to make you feel good. You need to know that."

"I appreciate that. And I only want you to feel good, too. Sorry I put a damper on the evening."

"That's okay," Alex said. "If you need me to take you home, I will. If you want to stay for dinner, you can. No pressure."

"I'd like to stay for dinner."

"Great."

"Are we going to continue the nude trend? Or shall we get dressed for dinner?"

"Let's get dressed," Alex said. "Or I might not be able to focus on the food."

They got dressed, and Alex handed Maggie a bottle of wine and two glasses.

"I thought I'd throw together a stir-fry if that's okay."

"Sounds good. What can I do to help?"

"Stand here with me and keep me company."

They chatted while Alex made dinner and then had another glass of wine while they ate.

"This is really good. You're quite the cook," Maggie said.

"Thanks. Do you cook?"

"No. It's not something I ever learned."

"Well, you do plenty of other things well." She winked.

Maggie blushed.

"Thanks."

They did the dishes, and it was getting late.

"I need to get you home, don't I?" Alex said.

"You really do."

"I always hate saying good-bye to you."

"I hate it, too."

"Maybe someday we won't have to? Maybe over one of your vacations, we can go away. Are you allowed to go on vacations?"

"I don't know. I mean, yeah, we can. I just never have. I usually stay close to the convent."

"Well, summer vacation is coming up, right?"

"Yeah."

"Keep it in mind."

"I will," Maggie said.

Chapter Six

Maggie and Alex fell into an easy routine. Every Sunday they spent long, lazy afternoons together making love and playing in the pool. The days were getting warmer, and summer vacation was just around the corner. Maggie was over at Alex's house. They were naked by the pool, relaxing in the sun.

"Hey, Mags," Alex said. "Do you remember when we talked about you going on vacation with me?"

"Yeah." Maggie's stomach churned a little bit. How would she explain to Reverend Mother the concept of going away with Alex?

"Well, I have an idea."

"Yeah? What's that?"

"I say we take a tour of Italy. We can even go to the Vatican. Would you like that?"

"Oh, my God," Maggie said. "That's like a Catholic's dream."

"I agree. Would you like to go? You can even call it a working vacation if you need to, somehow. I mean, if you need to convince the mother superior to let you go."

"But, Alex, I could never afford that."

"No, but I can. We can visit churches all over the country. And see the art. And maybe even go to Mass at the Vatican. Come on, what do you say?"

"Let me talk to Reverend Mother first?"

"Sure. I'm sure she'll be excited for you."

"I hope so."

"Now, let's go inside to celebrate."

They went to the master bedroom and lay on the bed. They made love slowly, tenderly. Alex ran her hand up and down Maggie's body. Maggie's skin rippled at her touch. She arched her hips, urging Alex to move her hand lower, between her legs, where she needed her. But Alex was in no hurry. Slowly, she dragged her hand down to Maggie's mons, then back up to her neck.

"You're driving me wild," Maggie said.

"Good."

"Are you going to touch me?"

"When I'm ready. I'm loving the feel of your skin. I love the way it responds to my touch."

"My whole body is responding to your touch. If you don't move that hand lower soon, I'm going to take care of myself without your help."

"Tsk tsk. Patience, my dear."

Alex bent and kissed Maggie's neck, nibbling and sucking as she did.

"Oh, dear God, Alex. Please."

"Okay, Mags. Okay."

Alex dragged her hand down Maggie's body again until it was between her legs.

"Oh, yes. That's it. Please."

She slipped her fingers inside Maggie, and Maggie arched to meet each thrust. She moved under her, urging her on.

"Does that feel good?" Alex said.

"Oh, God, yes. It feels so good."

"Tell me if you need more."

"I need more," Maggie said. "Please. Give me more."

Alex slid another finger inside, and Maggie felt fuller than she ever had. She threw her head back and screamed as Alex took her to one orgasm after another.

"Oh, my God," Maggie said when she'd caught her breath. "I don't know what you did, but that was the best ever."

"The best ever, huh? Well, I'll take that as a compliment."

"Now it's my turn to return the favor."

Maggie rolled on top of Alex and kissed her hard on her mouth. She moved off her and placed her hand between Alex's legs. She felt how hot and wet she was. It made Maggie dizzy with need. She slid her fingers inside Alex and stroked her. She moved faster and faster, coaxing Alex on. She rubbed her clit with her thumb, and Alex cried out, a low guttural yell that made Maggie swell with pride.

They lay together for a while before Alex suggested they go out to dinner.

"We're not staying in tonight?" Maggie said.

"I'm sorry. I forgot to pick anything up to eat. I was only focused on being with you."

"That's so sweet, but you don't have to take me out."

"But I want to. I want to take you to dinner. Is that really not okay?"

"No. It's fine. As long as you understand it's not necessary."

"I get that," Alex said. "I know nothing is necessary when I'm with you. I just like to do nice things for you, and I don't get to very often. So let me take you to dinner."

"Sounds good. Let's get dressed."

"Oh, yeah. There's that." Alex laughed. "If we must."

"Unfortunately, we must."

"Kiss me first," Alex said.

Maggie kissed her passionately and let her tongue wander into Alex's mouth. Alex returned the kiss in kind, and soon Alex had her hand between Maggie's legs again.

"Dinner can wait," she said.

Maggie spread her legs wider to allow Alex easier access. Alex rubbed her clit. She pressed it into Maggie's pubis, and Maggie cried out as the climax hit.

"Okay," Alex said. "Now we can get dressed."

They dressed quickly.

"What would you like for dinner?" Alex said.

"How about Mexican?"

"That sounds good to me."

They got in the truck, and Alex took Maggie's hand. Maggie smiled as they drove. She was so happy with their Sundays together. She couldn't get enough of her, and Sundays were filled with so much happiness.

They arrived at the restaurant, and Alex helped Maggie down out of her truck. She held on to Maggie's hand a little too long for Maggie's liking. She pulled away.

"Sorry," Alex said. "It's just so hard."

"I know. I know it is."

They walked into the restaurant and Maggie made sure to keep a safe distance between herself and Alex. She didn't want people talking. They were shown to their table. They read their menus, then set them down.

"You're so beautiful," Alex whispered.

Maggie blushed.

"Thank you," she said. "You're not so bad yourself."

"Thanks."

They sat in silence for a few minutes.

"So, will you talk to the mother superior about Italy? I'd really like to take you."

"Oh, definitely. I'll talk to her tomorrow. I promise."

"Great. I can get more information to you if you need it."

"Let me try with what we've got. I think she'll say okay. At least I hope so."

They ate their dinner in quiet conversation.

"This is so good," Maggie said. "I didn't realize how hungry I was."

"You worked up an appetite." She winked.

Maggie blushed.

"You're so bad," she said.

They finished dinner, and Alex paid the check. They walked out to the truck.

"It kills me, you know. That I can't hold your hand in public. It's like I've finally settled down and am with one woman and I can't let anyone know."

"No, you can't," Maggie said. "That would be horrible."

"I know. But what we have works for me so I shouldn't want more."

"Please don't."

"I won't."

Alex pulled into the parking lot at the convent.

"I had another great day," she said.

"Me, too. Thank you."

"I wish I could kiss you good night."

"Me, too, but you can't."

"Okay. So I'll just say good night and remind you to talk to the mother superior about Italy. I need to book the trip."

"Okay. I will. Good night, Alex."

"Good night."

Maggie crossed the garden and let herself in just before curfew. She got to her room and, as usual, threw herself on her bed and relived the moments of the day. She got up and took off her clothes and fell into a hard sleep.

The next day, Maggie went through her day to the best of her ability. She had a hard time focusing since she had promised Alex she'd talk to the mother superior after school. She hoped she'd say okay and not be suspicious.

School finally ended, and Maggie gathered up the homework to grade that evening. She walked to the convent and found Reverend Mother in her office, as expected. She looked up at Maggie.

"Hello, Maggie. Please, come in." She motioned to a chair across her desk. "What can I do for you?"

"Reverend Mother, I've been presented with the chance of a lifetime, and I want to ask your permission to say okay."

"A chance of a lifetime? What sort of chance?"

"Do you remember Alex Foster? You met her about a month ago after the coffee and doughnut social?"

"Yes. She comes to Mass every week. She seems like a good Catholic. Why?"

"She is going to take a tour of Italy this summer, including a visit to the Vatican. Reverend Mother, she's invited me to go with her. She'd pay for it. She doesn't want to go alone." Maggie heard herself lying to the mother superior and felt momentary guilt. But she really wanted to go.

"I think that would be wonderful. When would this happen?"

"It would be over summer vacation."

"Excellent. You deserve some time off, anyway. How long would the tour last?"

"I'm not sure how long. Maybe two or three weeks?"

"How exciting! I do hope you'll take lots of pictures to share."

"Yes, ma'am. Definitely."

"Well, you have my permission."

"Oh, thank you, Reverend Mother. Thank you so much."

"You're quite welcome."

Maggie practically skipped down the hall to her room. She opened a desk drawer and took out the phone slip she'd been given so long ago. She walked down the hall to a phone and dialed the number.

"Hello?" Alex said.

"Hello."

"Hey! What a surprise. Did you talk to the mother superior?"

"I did."

"And?"

"And she's all excited for me. She said okay."

"Most excellent. We'll look at the brochures Sunday and choose one of the tours, okay?"

"Sounds great. I'll see you then."

"Hey, Mags? I miss you."

"You, too."

Alex laughed.

"Okay. I'll see you Sunday."

The week dragged on for Maggie. She couldn't wait for Sunday to see Alex again. She did her best to focus on her class, but it wasn't easy. Friday was a test day, which gave her too much time alone with her thoughts. Saturday she spent tending to the garden to keep herself occupied.

"You've done such a nice job out here," Mother Superior said. Maggie hadn't heard her approach.

"Thank you. I do enjoy it."

"Everything looks beautiful. Now, you should get cleaned up. It's almost time for dinner."

Maggie was surprised at how late it had gotten. She'd had no idea it was almost dinner time. She hurried to the shower, which was empty at that hour. As the water washed over her, she thought of Alex's caresses and almost gave in to the urge to touch herself. She didn't, though, as she didn't have much time and there was no guarantee nobody would walk in on her. She finished her shower, got dressed, and headed down to the dining room.

Sunday morning, Maggie woke early and dressed for Mass. She went to the eight thirty Mass to pray undisturbed and to thank God for giving her the opportunity to travel to Italy. She went again to the eleven o'clock Mass since that's the one Alex always attended. When she saw her walk in, Maggie's heart thumped in her chest. Alex looked handsome as ever in blue slacks and a light blue button-down shirt. Maggie couldn't see from where she stood, but she knew Alex's eyes would look gorgeous with that outfit.

After Mass, she crossed the church to see Alex, rather than head to the social. She was right, Alex's eyes shone.

"You look very nice," she said.

"Thanks," Alex said. "So do you."

"Aw. That's sweet of you to say. You've seen me in this outfit thousands of times."

"Maybe, but I still think you look nice. Shouldn't you be working the coffee and doughnut social?"

"I'm on my way. Are you coming?"

"I'll pop in for a few. Why not?"

They crossed to the parish hall together. Maggie was so aware of Alex's presence beside her, she wondered if her feelings showed on her face. She hoped not. The last thing she needed was a scandal. She probably should have thought of that before she started seeing Alex. Seeing? Is that what she was doing? Sure, it was more than just sleeping together, wasn't it?

These thoughts swirled through her head as she entered the hall. She shook them away and walked with Alex to the doughnut table. She grabbed a doughnut then turned to face her.

"Don't worry about me," Alex said. "I'll be fine. You go mingle."

Maggie left her standing there and made her way around the room. She visited families as usual and spent some time talking to some older parishioners. She felt like she'd had a good hour when it was time to clean up.

As was the norm now, Alex helped out.

"I thought you were only staying for a few," Maggie said when she saw that Alex was still there.

"I thought I was, but I ended up talking to your mother superior. She wanted to know all about the trip. I think she's more excited than we are."

"As if that's possible."

Alex laughed.

"I know."

They finished up and walked back to the convent.

"You think your mother superior suspects anything?" Alex said.

"I can't imagine why she would. We're just good friends as far as she can tell."

"I hope you're right."

"She has no reason to think anything else. Believe me."

They arrived at her room, and Maggie changed into shorts and a T-shirt. She slipped on her sandals, grabbed her suit just for show, and was ready to go.

"Let's get out of here," she said.

"Works for me."

They held hands as they drove to Alex's house. The familiar feel of Alex's hand in Maggie's warmed her heart. She loved her hands, loved the way they felt on her and inside her. She blushed at her train of thought.

Alex glanced over at her.

"What are you thinking about?"

"Nothing."

"Don't lie to me," she teased her. "You're bright red so I know you were thinking something juicy."

"If you must know, I was thinking how much I like your hands."

"Odd, but why would that make you blush?"

"Because I like everything you do with your hands?"

"Huh? Oh! The light bulb just went on." She laughed. "I'm glad you enjoy them."

Maggie blushed deeper red and kept her mouth shut the rest of the trip.

Chapter Seven

As usual, once the door closed behind them, they were in each other's arms. Maggie loved the feel of Alex's strong arms around her, the feel of her lips on her own. She leaned into her, felt Alex's breasts press into hers, and she grew light-headed.

"Swim time or play time first?" Alex said.

"I need you, Alex. Please. Take me."

"Gladly." She took her hand and led her to the guest bedroom. She slowly and purposefully undressed Maggie until she stood naked before her. Maggie shifted self-consciously under Alex's scrutiny.

"You're magnificent," Alex said.

"I'm naked," Maggie said. "Shouldn't you be, too?"

"Oh, yeah." Alex quickly stripped out of her clothes. "Now we're even."

"Hold me."

"Gladly."

Alex pulled Maggie to her, and they pressed together, flesh to flesh.

"You feel so wonderful," Maggie said.

"So do you."

"I need you to take me now."

"Lie down."

Maggie lay on the bed, and Alex climbed up next to her. She stared longingly at Maggie's body, and Maggie blushed under the scrutiny.

"Are you going to do more than just look?" Maggie said.

"All in due time. Patience, my dear."

Alex ran her hand over the length of Maggie's body. Maggie's skin rippled at her touch. She moved her hand lower and skimmed the warm wetness between her legs. Maggie spread her legs wider to allow for easier access. Alex delved inside her and stroked all her favorite spots. She dragged her thumb over Maggie's clit and sent Maggie into orbit. When she'd finally come down, Alex lay next to her, smiling at her.

"That was wonderful," Maggie said. She slid down between Alex's legs. "You're beautiful."

She lowered her head and tasted Alex. She tasted divine, salty and musky. She had a flavor that haunted Maggie. She thrust her tongue inside Alex as deep as it would go and lapped at all the juices flowing there. Alex arched off the bed to urge her on. Maggie needed no encouragement. She continued to lick deep inside her until her tongue hurt. Then she moved to Alex's clit and sucked it between her lips. She ran her tongue over it. Alex pressed into the back of her head and held her in place. Maggie kept at it until Alex arched off the bed, froze, and cried out Maggie's name.

Satiated, they lay together for a few minutes until Alex's excitement could wait no more.

"We really should look at those brochures I brought home," she said. "The ones about Italy."

"Oh, yeah. Let's do that."

Alex brought them into the bedroom so they could look at them.

"These all look wonderful," Maggie said. "I especially like this one."

She held the brochure showing a tour that took them from Rome to Milan, including trips to Venice and Florence.

"That was my favorite, too," Alex said. "You know, Mags, I was thinking. We don't have to do a tour if you don't want. We could see the same places if we fly to Rome and rent a car."

"That sounds like fun, but how would we be sure we were seeing everything we want to?"

"We're smart women. We could find our way around."

"Still, I think a tour might be better."

"We couldn't be open on a tour. Especially since everyone would know you're a nun."

"Let's Google driving in Italy," Maggie suggested.

"Okay."

They went into Alex's office and googled it.

"Italians are crazy drivers, and I don't recommend driving in the big cities or on the Amalfi Coast."

"Hm," Alex said. "Perhaps you're right. We should just go on a tour."

"Great. Now that that's decided, all we have to do is book our tour."

"I'll do it tomorrow. Maybe we can have dinner tomorrow night at Mama Italiano's to celebrate?"

"I'll ask Reverend Mother. I don't think it will be a problem."

"Right on. Now come here and let me kiss you."

Maggie stood from the desk chair and stepped into Alex's embrace. Alex kissed her fiercely, and Maggie responded in kind. She felt Alex's hand roam over her body and her skin was on fire. Alex slipped her hand between Maggie's legs and stroked her. Maggie fought to maintain her balance. She gripped Alex and held on for dear life as one orgasm after another crashed through her body.

"You okay?" Alex said.

"Give me a minute," Maggie said as she caught her breath. "Okay. I think I'm good now. I think I can trust my legs."

"Great. Now, let's hit the pool."

They swam laps together before Maggie took her usual spot on the steps to watch Alex finish hers. Alex finally came over to join her.

"So, what day does school get out for you?" Alex said.

"June third."

"Oh, so just over a month from now. Great. So, we'll find a tour that leaves in June. That'll be great."

"Yes, it will. I can't wait to go on our great adventure."

MJ WILLIAMZ

They relaxed in the pool until five o'clock rolled around.

"I don't know about you," Alex said. "But I'm getting hungry."

"Me, too. We've been working up our appetites today, haven't we?"

"That we have. I have a couple of steaks to grill. Sound good?"

"Sounds heavenly. I'll get the wine."

Maggie brought out two glasses of wine and handed one to Alex who was manning the grill.

"Thanks," Alex said and took a sip. "This is just what I needed."

Maggie sat at the patio table and watched Alex. She admired how easy she was in her own skin. Maggie still got shy about being naked around her all the time, but Alex never showed any discomfort. She was so confident and comfortable with herself. It made Maggie smile.

"What are you thinking about?" Alex had turned to look at her.

"Just you."

"Yeah? What about me?"

"Just how confident you are. It's like an aphrodisiac to me."

"Well, good. As long as you're thinking happy thoughts like that, I'm okay."

"You're much better than okay, my dear."

"Thanks," Alex said. "Now, do you mind grabbing a couple of plates? These babies are ready."

Maggie went to the kitchen and took two plates out of the cupboard. She grabbed silverware from the drawer and the salad from the fridge. She loved how familiar she was with Alex's place. It felt like a second home to her. She took everything out to the patio.

"Thanks," Alex said again. "I could have gotten the salad."

"No worries. I carried it all just fine."

They sat at the patio table and enjoyed their dinner and another glass of wine each. When they were through, they worked together to get things cleaned up.

"I think it's time to go back to bed," Alex said.

"You don't have to ask me twice."

This time, they went upstairs to the master bedroom. The bed was bigger and it was Alex's room, so it smelled and felt like her. Maggie loved that room.

Alex pulled Maggie into a tight embrace. Their skin together was heaven for Maggie. She loved every inch of Alex and wondered at how well they fit together. They kissed, but it was slow and deliberate, as was their lovemaking after.

Maggie lay on the bed and reached out her hand, beckoning Alex to join her. Alex climbed up with her and held her close.

"I love how you feel in my arms," Alex said.

"I love being in your arms."

"That's a good thing."

Alex kissed her again, another deep and passionate kiss that captured Maggie's soul. Maggie responded in kind, and Alex unwrapped her arms from her and ran her hand slowly over Maggie's body.

"Your touch makes me crazy," Maggie said.

"Good."

"But I need more. Please."

"Okay, Mags, okay." She slid her hand between Maggie's legs and slowly stroked her.

"I feel like I'm going to explode," Maggie said. "Please, Alex, don't tease me."

Alex rubbed Maggie's clit hard and fast until Maggie cried out as she climaxed.

Maggie then moved her hand down to where Alex's legs met. She slipped her fingers inside her then pulled them out before delving deeper. Alex arched off the bed and met each thrust.

"Oh, God, Maggie. Oh yes, that's it."

Maggie continued what she was doing until Alex called her name as she came.

They lay together and dozed. Maggie woke up first and looked at the clock. It was nine fifteen.

"Hey." She shook Alex's shoulder. "Hey, wake up. We need to get me home."

Alex looked at her with heavy lids.

"Huh?"

"I need to get home. I don't want to miss curfew."

"Okay, okay," Alex said. She sat up. Her eyes were more focused. "Okay. Let's get dressed and I'll drive you home."

They dressed in silence and got in the truck.

"You okay to drive?" Maggie said.

"Sure. I'm awake now. Though, it sure was nice snuggling and sleeping with you."

"Yes, it was."

They arrived at the convent.

"So, you'll make the reservations tomorrow?" Maggie said.

"I promise. And I'll pick you up at six for dinner. If that won't work, you have my number."

"That I do. Good night, Alex."

"Good night, Maggie."

The next day, Maggie threw herself into her teaching, determined not to be distracted. She still had a month to go until the end of the year and decided to buck up and deal with it. The day went off without a hitch, and after she had loaded all her homework into her briefcase, she headed back to the convent. She went directly to Reverend Mother's office.

"Hello, Maggie. To what do I owe this visit?"

"I had a couple of things I wanted to discuss with you."

"Certainly. You have my undivided attention." She folded her hands on top of the paperwork on her desk.

"Well, first of all, I wanted to know if I could miss dinner tonight? I'm supposed to meet with Alex Foster to learn about the trip to Italy. She's supposed to book it today. Oh, and I also wanted to let you know the tour only lasts eight days, not weeks like I had originally thought."

"I'm still so excited about your vacation, my dear. I can't wait to see pictures when you return. And, yes, you may skip dinner tonight. But, Maggie?"

"Yes?"

"Don't let this become the norm. This is twice now. I don't want to see you getting into the habit of missing dinners."

"Yes, ma'am."

"Okay. You may go then. Have fun and let me know what your plans are when they're finalized."

"Will do. Good night, Mother Superior."

"Good night, Maggie."

Maggie went back to her room and graded papers until five fifty-five. At that time, she walked through the gardens to the parking lot. Alex was already there. She climbed into Alex's truck and smiled broadly.

"It's such a treat to see you on days other than Sunday," she said.

"Believe me, I know what you mean. Waiting during the week drives me crazy."

"I know. I'm sorry that it's so hard."

"It's okay. I knew when I first committed to you what I was in for. Nothing's changed. I get it."

"Thank you."

Alex reached out and took Maggie's hand.

"Thank you. So, did you talk to your mother superior about our trip some more?"

"I did. I told her I'll know the details tonight, but I told her it was only an eight-day tour. I'd originally thought it would be a couple of weeks, at least."

"We could have taken our time if we'd opted to drive, but I would be scared to after what we read. So I'm glad we're going this route."

"Me, too. So did you book everything today?"

"I did. We leave June nineteenth."

"Yay. I'm so excited!"

"So am I, Mags. So am I."

They pulled into the restaurant parking lot, and Alex loosened her grip on Maggie's hand so they could get out. They entered the restaurant and were shown to their seats.

"I love this place," Alex said. "I hope you don't mind my wanting to come here again."

"Not at all. And what better place to celebrate our Italian vacation?"

"I agree."

They ordered their dinners and sat back and gazed at each other.

"I've missed you," Alex said.

"You just saw me yesterday."

"I know. But still…"

"You're so sweet."

"Thank you. I only say the truth," Alex said.

"You look very nice today." Maggie took in Alex's deep blue golf shirt that set off her eyes.

"Thank you. So do you."

"I can't believe I didn't change out of my teaching outfit today. Normally, the first thing I do when I get to my room is change."

"Well, I'm glad you didn't. You look so pretty all dressed up."

"Does that mean I don't when I'm in my casual clothes?"

Alex laughed.

"No. That decidedly does not mean that. Heck, you look good in nothing."

Maggie blushed.

"I'm glad you think so."

"Let's finish our dinner so we can get out of here."

They ate their meals in easy conversation, and when they were through, hurried to the truck to head to Alex's. Maggie's stomach was fluttering, she was so excited. She couldn't wait to be with Alex. A Monday tryst was special, and she was ready to enjoy it.

When they got to the house, they made their way directly to the guest room on the first floor. They needed each other immediately, and it was the closest place. They stripped and fell onto the bed, limbs intertwined, tongues frolicking over each other. Maggie's hormones flared.

She moved her hand between Alex's legs and stroked her lovingly. She thrust her fingers inside her and moved them in and out over and over. Alex bucked off the bed, meeting every thrust. Maggie withdrew her fingers and pressed them into Alex's clit. Alex called her name as the orgasms washed over her.

"Whatever happened to ladies first?" Alex grinned when she'd caught her breath.

"Not today. I needed you and decided to have you."

"Well, I need you now."

Alex kissed down Maggie until she was between her legs. She licked the length of her.

"You taste so good," she said.

"Thank you."

Alex dipped her tongue inside Maggie and lapped at her walls. She tried to suck up all the juices that were flowing there, but more kept flowing. She licked and sucked and devoured Maggie. She sucked on her lips and ran her tongue between them. Maggie groaned, the orgasm forming deep inside her. She could feel it building. She blocked out all thoughts and allowed herself only to feel what Alex was doing. She focused on it as the climax neared. The orgasms started then and racked her body again and again.

CHAPTER EIGHT

The next month passed quickly for Maggie. The kids were amped for their summer vacation, but she figured they couldn't be anywhere near as excited as she was. They grew restless, and it was with great pleasure that Maggie dismissed them for their vacation.

When the kids were gone, Maggie went back to her room and worked on their grades. She had a week to get them to Reverend Mother, but she wanted to get them done and out of the way. She wanted to focus all her attention on preparing for her trip to Italy.

She got her grades all entered and handed them off to Reverend Mother and checked her wardrobe for clothes appropriate for her upcoming vacation. She figured she could wear shorts and T-shirts for the bulk of the time and wear skirts and blouses at the Vatican or other cathedrals they happened to visit.

Sunday before their holiday, Maggie and Alex spent their day out by the pool.

"I can't believe we leave this Wednesday night," Maggie said. "And that the tour starts on Friday. I'm so excited. I can't believe it's finally here."

"I know exactly what you mean. Imagine, Mags, we get to spend nine nights together away from prying eyes."

"I hear you. It's going to be heaven."

After they had dried off in the sun, they went inside and made love in Alex's bed. Alex took Maggie to new heights that day, and

Maggie returned the favor. When they were satiated, they dressed and began the now familiar routine of making dinner.

Maggie served the wine while Alex grilled. Then she brought the salad, plates, and silverware out when Alex declared the meat was ready. Maggie liked their routine. She enjoyed everything about the time she spent with Alex. And she couldn't wait until their vacation to spend ten full days with her alone.

Wednesday morning, Maggie woke early and prayed for a safe trip. She prayed to God to let her learn as much as she could through their travels and to keep them safe in the unfamiliar country. She crossed herself and stood.

Maggie checked the time. It was only eight o'clock. She walked to the dining room and met Reverend Mother, who was having breakfast.

"You must be so excited," Reverend Mother said.

"I truly am. I can't wait to get going. Alex is going to pick me up this afternoon, and I'm already filled with jitters. It will be a long flight, but it will be so worth it. I can't wait to explore Italy."

"You're very blessed, my child, to have this opportunity."

"I realize this. I'm so lucky Alex chose me to accompany her."

"You really are."

Maggie didn't feel like talking any more about Alex to Reverend Mother. She was overcome with guilt, which was the last thing she wanted to feel as she prepared to embark on the trip of a lifetime. She walked over to the breakfast bar and made some waffles and grabbed some fruit. Fortunately, as she did this, Reverend Mother left the dining room.

She ate in peace and quiet, as was her preference. She had often questioned this trip and what it would mean to the vows she broke every week. She hoped to gain guidance while in Italy. She had been questioning her calling and wondering if she should drop out of the convent. She hoped this trip would solidify her decision one way or another.

At three o'clock, Maggie grabbed her suitcase and walked through the gardens to the parking lot. Alex was already there waiting for her.

"Hey, beautiful," Alex said when Maggie had stowed her bag and climbed into the truck.

"Hey yourself." Maggie was all smiles. "How's your day going?"

"Not bad. I worked a little this morning. Only until noon, though. I needed to do something to keep myself occupied."

"I wish I'd had something to do. I mostly paced in my room." She laughed.

"Well, let's go back to my place and kill some time. I know just what we need."

"I'm sure you do."

They got to Alex's house, and Alex let them in. She took Maggie's hand and pulled her into a warm embrace.

"You doing okay?" she said.

"I am. Just excited. And maybe a little nervous."

"What's to be nervous about?"

"Flying. I've only flown a few times. The idea of an eighteen-hour flight rather terrifies me, to be honest."

"Nonsense. It'll be fine. Come on in the kitchen. I bought some champagne to celebrate."

"Oh, that sounds wonderful," Maggie said. "Let's have some."

Alex popped the top and poured them each a flute.

"To Italy," she said.

"To Italy."

They toasted and sipped the champagne. Maggie thought it was delicious. She could feel herself relaxing after the first glass. When Alex poured the second glass, they walked out to the patio to enjoy it in the sun.

"It's a beautiful day to start this trip," Alex said.

"It really is. It's gorgeous out here."

"Did you want to go for a swim? We have plenty of time."

"Maybe. Let's finish the champagne first."

They sipped the champagne in comfortable silence. Maggie loved the feel of the sun on her face and knew she'd want to play in the pool soon. She finished her glass and stood. She stripped off her clothes and headed toward the water.

"So, I guess a swim is in order," Alex said.

"Yes, it is."

Maggie took her spot on the second step and relaxed in the warm water. It felt good lapping against her bare skin. A shadow fell over her, and she looked up to see Alex climbing in next to her.

"Mind if I join you?" Alex said.

"Please do."

"You're so beautiful sitting here. I wonder sometimes what you're thinking. You get this far-off look, but it only adds to your beauty."

"Why, thank you. I was simply marveling at how good the sun and the water feel."

"Yeah. It's a good combination."

Alex rested her hand on Maggie's thigh.

"I need you, Maggie," she said. "I need you now."

"Take me, then. I'm yours, Alex. Take me anytime you want."

Alex slid her hand up Maggie's thigh. Maggie shivered at her touch. Alex moved closer to her center. Maggie spread her legs wide. Alex slipped her fingers inside Maggie and Maggie gasped.

"Oh, God. You feel so good."

"Mm. So do you. You're so tight and hot and wet. I love the feel of you."

"Don't just sit there, Alex. Move them in and out. Take care of me."

Alex did just as she was asked. She moved her fingers in and out of Maggie, thrusting them deeper each time. Maggie threw her head back and closed her eyes. She focused on nothing but Alex's fingers. Alex delved deeper still, and Maggie clenched her teeth to keep from screaming out loud as she climaxed over and over again. Alex slowly withdrew her hand.

"You ready to swim some laps now?" she said.

"Give me a minute to recuperate."

"No problem. I'm going to start swimming. You join me when you're ready."

But Maggie wasn't ready. Nor would she be that day. She was content to relax on the step and watch Alex's trim figure slice through the water. She was becoming aroused again just watching her.

When Alex finished, she sat on the step next to Maggie again. Maggie waited until her breathing was normal, then kissed her. She kissed her passionately with all her need poured into the kiss. When the kiss ended, Alex was breathless again.

"I need you," Maggie said.

Alex climbed out of the water and sat on the edge of the pool with her legs dangling in the water.

"Take me, then. Have at me, Mags. I need you, too."

Maggie stood in the water and walked over to where Alex sat, legs spread wide, her womanhood clearly visible and calling to Maggie. Maggie bent to taste her. There was her familiar flavor mixed with chlorine. It wasn't a bad combination, and Maggie lapped at her, loving the flavors. She sucked her lips and ran her tongue between them before focusing on her hard clit. She sucked it between her lips and flicked it with her tongue. Alex pressed Maggie's face into her, and Maggie fought for breath while she worked on Alex's clit.

Finally, Alex froze, then released her grip on Maggie and fell back, limp, on the concrete.

"You're going to burn yourself on that hot concrete," Maggie said.

"It's not that hot," Alex murmured.

"If you say so."

Alex soon sat up straight and looked down at Maggie.

"You're something else, you know that, woman?"

"So are you."

"Thanks."

"You ready for something to eat?"

"I am," Maggie said.

They ate quietly and then went upstairs to Alex's room where they made love again. When they'd both had enough, Maggie rolled over and looked at the clock.

"We should get going. We need to be at the airport soon."

They dressed and hurried to the airport, where they waited only a few minutes before boarding the plane to take them to LAX and then to Rome.

The flight from Los Angeles to Rome was long but uneventful. They talked and slept and talked some more. Maggie loved resting her head on Alex's shoulder to sleep. It felt so right. When they finally landed, it was late Thursday evening in Rome. Alex flagged a taxi that took them to the Albani Hotel where the tour would be staying. They stored their luggage in their room and headed down to the restaurant for dinner and drinks.

They dined on traditional Mediterranean cuisine and enjoyed delicious red wine.

"So far, so good, huh, Maggie?" Alex said.

"So far, so wonderful."

"And it's only going to get better."

"I know. I can't wait."

After dinner, they went back to their room and christened their bed. They were both exhausted when they were through and they had decided to get up early the next morning to grab some breakfast before exploring the city a little on their own. They weren't scheduled to meet the tour until five, which gave them plenty of time to sightsee.

Maggie woke Friday morning to Alex between her legs. She moaned her approval and pressed Alex's face into her as she came fully awake.

"Oh, my God. That feels so good."

She moved all over the bed as she ground herself into Alex. She finally felt a knot of energy coalesce deep inside her. She focused only on Alex and the energy. Finally, the knot unwound and shot electrical currents all over her body as she climaxed.

"Good morning to me," she said.

"Mm." Alex climbed up next to her. "Good morning to us."

"I like this sleeping with you business."

"I thought you might."

Maggie moved lower and took her place between Alex's legs. She licked and sucked on everything she saw and was rewarded when Alex called out her name.

"Let's hit the shower now," Alex said. She took Maggie's hand and led her into the bathroom. She turned on the water and pulled Maggie close to her while they waited for it to heat up. "I can't get enough of your body."

"I can't get enough of yours, either. We're so right together."

"Yes, we are."

They climbed into the shower and lathered each other up. Alex slid her hand between Maggie's legs and coaxed one, then another orgasm out of her. Maggie dropped to her knees and buried her face between Alex's legs. She returned the favor.

When they were both steady on their feet again, they rinsed off and got out of the shower. They dried off and dressed in shorts and T-shirts. Maggie slipped on her Birkenstocks, and Alex wore tennis shoes.

"You sure you'll be okay walking in those?" Alex said.

"Sure. They're the most comfortable shoes I've ever owned."

"Okay then. Let's go get breakfast and then start our adventure."

They enjoyed the breakfast buffet until they thought they'd explode.

"Good thing we're going to be walking around," Maggie said. "We so need to burn off that breakfast."

"Yeah, we do."

"So what's our first stop?"

"Villa Borghese Art Gallery and Gardens. I made the reservations the other day. We shouldn't have any trouble getting in."

"Oh, yeah. Let's go. I can't wait to see them."

They went to the gallery first and enjoyed works of art by Bernini, Rubens, Raphael, Titian, and Caravaggio. Maggie had always loved art and had even taken a history of art class at Cal Poly. She was in love with the paintings she saw there. She recognized several from her class years ago.

Then they went to the gardens. It was the third largest park in Rome. It was a former vineyard that had been turned into the extensive gardens. There were villas throughout that had more art on display.

"You're loving this, aren't you?" Alex said.

"I really am. Are you?"

"I'm with you. How could I not be?"

"You're so sweet," Maggie said.

"I mean it, Mags. I love spending time with you."

"Thanks. I love spending time with you, too."

They spent several hours there, then made their way back to the hotel for a late lunch. Everything else they wanted to see would be included in the tour. After lunch, they went to their room. Once they were inside, Alex pulled Maggie to her and kissed her passionately. Maggie returned the kiss with a fierceness that surprised herself.

Alex walked Maggie back to the bed and eased her down, so she sat on it. Alex removed Maggie's sandals, her shorts, and her shirt. She pulled her underwear off and unhooked her bra. She tossed everything over the back of a chair and stood gazing down at Maggie.

Maggie dragged her fingers lazily between her legs.

"Oh, no you don't," Alex said. "That's my job."

She quickly stripped and climbed onto the bed with Maggie. She ran her hand over Maggie.

"Your skin is so soft," she said. "I love it."

She moved her hand between her legs. Maggie was wet and ready for her. She slid her fingers inside, and Maggie moved against her in perfect rhythm. Maggie wrapped her arms tight around Alex and screamed as the orgasms racked her body.

Maggie moved down between Alex's legs and lapped at her juices. She thrust her tongue as deep as it would go inside her and licked her satin walls. She licked her way to Alex's clit and sucked on it until Alex called her name as she climaxed.

They lay together and dozed briefly.

"Come on, sleepyhead," Alex said. "We should shower and dress for dinner. It's almost time to meet the tour."

"I'm awake," Maggie said.

They took a shower together, where they brought each other to several more orgasms then got dressed. It was time to go to the restaurant and meet the tour.

Chapter Nine

They got downstairs at precisely five o'clock and saw a group of people gathered around a woman holding a sign that indicated their tour group. They wandered over to the woman and introduced themselves. She checked them off her list.

"I'm Teresa," she said. "I'll be your tour guide."

"So nice to meet you," Maggie said.

"It's nice to meet you, too. I do hope you'll enjoy the tour."

"I'm sure we will."

"Now go take your place with the others. We'll leave for dinner in just a few minutes."

Maggie and Alex joined the others. There were people of all ages in the group, from twenty-somethings to geriatrics.

"This should be fun," Maggie said, though her stomach was in knots. Spending so much time with total strangers would be new to her, but she didn't know why she was so nervous about it. Probably because these people would only know her as Maggie, Alex's traveling companion. Not as Sister Mary Margaret the nun.

"Okay, everyone," Teresa called. "Time to go to the restaurant. We have several tables reserved for us, so find them and get situated."

Maggie and Alex were seated at a table with four others. They were of the geriatric generation, and Maggie was keen to learn all she could from them. Dinner passed with pleasant conversation. The two couples they were with were from Wisconsin, a place

Maggie had never been. She listened attentively to their stories, and soon dinner was over.

Teresa moved through the tables, chatting with each group as she did. She got to their table and told them that now that dinner was over, they could do a little sightseeing on their own, or they could just retire for the evening. Morning would come early, and the tour would start in earnest.

Maggie and Alex approached Teresa after the rest of the crowd had filed out.

"We're looking for a place to go dancing," Alex said. "One that caters to women."

"You should try the Vicious," Teresa said. "It doesn't cater to women specifically, but it's the 'it' place and it's very gay friendly. I highly recommend it."

"Thanks," Alex said. "We'll check it out."

"Don't stay out too late, though. You've got a big day ahead of you tomorrow."

"We won't."

Maggie and Alex went up to their room to change into appropriate clothes to go to the club. They had a couple of hours to kill so, rather than get dressed right away, they fell into bed together where they explored each other's bodies as if they'd never met before. Alex spent extra time with Maggie, exploring every nook and cranny. She made sure no part of her was untouched or unloved. Maggie came over and over again to Alex's skilled fingers.

Maggie loved Alex's body with extra care. She made sure to kiss, suck, or lick every inch of her. Alex cried out as Maggie brought her to several orgasms. They took another shower, a long one where they continued to please each other until they were both exhausted from climaxing so much. They got out of the shower and dried off. They dressed for their night on the town and went downstairs.

They took a taxi and arrived at the club on Via Achille Grandi. It was rockin' when they got there at just past midnight.

They walked downstairs into the dark bar. It wasn't very big, but it was hard to tell just how big it was with all the mirrors on the walls. They cut through the crowd to get their drinks. With cocktails in hand, they wandered into another room from where the music was coming. The music was techno, a sound they had both heard before. Not from their generation by far, they still managed to dance and have fun. It was standing room only in the small room, but they moved and grooved and signaled to the waitress when they wanted more drinks.

After a couple of hours, Maggie pleaded exhaustion and Alex agreed that it was time to get back to the hotel to get some sleep. They lay down, intending to sleep, but the sight of Alex's naked body next to her got Maggie going again. She kissed Alex hard on her mouth before kissing down to take a nipple into her mouth. She moved lower down her body until she was comfortably between her legs. She lapped at the length of her, savoring the flavor that was all Alex. She continued to work her magic until Alex cried out.

"No more, Maggie. I can't take anymore," she said.

"Okay. We should get some sleep anyway."

"Not until I've had you."

Alex slid her hand down Maggie's body and slipped her fingers easily inside her. She stroked deep inside and ran her fingers along her walls. She found the soft spot that made Maggie lose her mind. She continued to rub it until Maggie climaxed on her hand. She moved up next to Maggie.

"Now, we can get some sleep," she said.

They were up early the next morning.

"How are you feeling?" Alex said.

"I'm excited. Too excited to be tired. How about you?"

"About the same."

"Good. Shall we take a shower?"

"We shall. Let me make a pot of coffee first."

Maggie turned the shower on to let it warm up. It was nice and hot when Alex came in.

"You ready?" Maggie said.

"Always." Alex moved her eyebrows up and down and smiled.

They made love in the shower until they had had enough. Then they got out, dressed, had coffee, and headed downstairs to meet the tour group for breakfast. They ate with a couple of young kids in their mid-twenties. They were from North Carolina. It was a fun breakfast with more exchanging of stories. Their stomachs were full when Teresa announced it was time to get on the bus to start their day.

Their first stop was at the Vatican Museums. The group gathered around the ball in front of the museums.

"You're free to wander around. You have two hours. Enjoy everything you see. I'll see you all back out here in two hours."

Maggie and Alex checked their watches. Two hours.

"Do you think that'll be enough time to see everything?" Maggie said to Alex.

"I don't know, but we'd better get started."

They walked into the building with its high vaulted ceilings and art on display everywhere. They checked out all the paintings and sculptures they had time to. They were mesmerized by the sheer talent on display there.

"This place is amazing," Maggie said.

"No doubt. What's your favorite?"

"I liked all the sculptures. The paintings were wonderful, too, but I really liked the sculptures. I couldn't possibly choose a favorite."

"Good. I'm glad you're enjoying yourself."

They walked out into the Rome heat and walked to the ball to meet the rest of the group. Everyone was chattering about what they'd seen and what they'd liked most.

"I think two hours was the perfect amount of time, don't you?" Maggie said.

"I do. I don't know that we could have seen anything more."

Teresa showed up and they walked together the short distance to the Sistine Chapel. Maggie was in awe as she stared up at the ceiling.

"This is beautiful," she said.

"Yeah, it is."

"Do you know that there are stories from the Bible depicted up there?"

"So, I've heard."

"It's just so awesome. It's almost overwhelming."

"Just relax," Alex said. "Take in what you can. Don't try to take in too much."

"Oh, look." Maggie pointed. "It's the *Last Judgement*."

"I see. It's magnificent."

"Oh, yes. It truly is."

They wandered through the chapel, taking in the paintings on all the walls. Maggie felt a familiar stir inside her at religious work. She felt drawn to it. She couldn't explain her feelings, but she felt at home in the chapel. She could only imagine how she'd feel in the actual Vatican.

The next stop was St. Peter's Square and Basilica.

"Look at it," Maggie said reverently. "Just look at it."

"I know, Mags. I know. It's amazing, truly amazing."

The Italian Renaissance architecture was truly awe-inspiring.

"And there's the obelisk," Maggie said.

"What's the meaning of that?"

"It's where St. Peter was crucified. Or so the legend goes."

"Wow."

They entered the basilica and followed the tour group to the first chapel of the north aisle where they saw Michelangelo's *Pieta.*

"Oh, my God," Maggie gasped. "It's incredible. Look at how he captured Mary's face. She looks so peaceful holding her son. It is so lifelike."

"It is."

Maggie felt a strong stir now that she was in the Vatican. This was the headquarters of the Catholic Church. This is where she belonged. How could she have ever thought of giving up her sisterhood? She was a nun. She belonged serving the Church.

"Come on," Teresa was saying. "Let's go to the next chapel."

When they were all gathered around her by the altar, she went on.

"Under this altar is the final resting place of Pope John Paul the Second."

Maggie bent her knee and genuflected in front of the altar. She made the sign of the cross before she stood.

Alex glanced at her. Maggie met her gaze and smiled. How could she tell her everything she was feeling? She was fighting tears, she was so moved by her experience. She followed Teresa through the rest of the tour, lost in the amazement she was feeling.

"Come along," Teresa said. "Time for the next step of our tour, the Coliseum."

Maggie tore herself away from the Vatican slowly. She didn't want to leave. She wanted to stay there all day, maybe longer. She truly felt at home there. She was quiet on the ride to the Coliseum.

"You okay?" Alex said. "I'm worried about you."

"I'm fine. That was just such an overwhelming experience. I'm just trying to process it all."

"Okay. As long as you're doing all right."

"I am. I'm sorry. I'll try to get out of my head. I need to be present for you this trip."

"You need to do whatever you need to do. I'm fine. I'm having a blast."

"Oh, good."

Alex reached out and gave Maggie's hand a squeeze. She let go and turned to listen to Teresa describe places they passed.

They arrived at the Coliseum and filed inside. Teresa described the history of the building, including gladiator battles and explained how those condemned to death would be sent into the arena, naked and unarmed, to face the beasts of death which would tear them to pieces.

Maggie shivered at the thought and Alex wrapped her arm around her. Maggie leaned into her, weak with the idea of all those souls dying such a terrible death.

The last stop on the tour that day was the Roman Forum.

"This place was originally a marketplace," Teresa said. "And most important businesses were located around this back in the ancient days."

Maggie and Alex wandered the ruins with the rest of them.

"Okay," Teresa said. "It's time to get back to the hotel. Today's tour is over. For those of you who bought the side tour, your guide will meet you at the hotel in an hour."

"I'm famished," Maggie said when they got off the bus.

"I agree. Let's go get some lunch and then we'll go on our side tour."

They ate lunch in easy conversation.

"So, you really enjoyed everything you saw today, didn't you?" Alex said.

"Oh, I did. Did you feel it in the Vatican? The feeling inside it? As a Catholic, I felt so close to everything there."

"I felt it, too, Mags. It was a strong pull at something deep inside."

"Oh, thank God you understand. I'm so glad you felt it, too."

"I did. No worries there."

When they finished their meal, they went out to the lobby to look for their tour guide. They found him, a nice man named Marco. They got on another bus and drove to the Spanish Steps, the Trevi Fountain, and the Pantheon. It was a wonderful afternoon, and Maggie and Alex were exhausted when they got back to the hotel.

"Do you want to take a nap?" Maggie said.

"I'd like to sleep with you." Alex grinned.

"That sounds nice."

"Yeah?"

"Yeah."

"Let's get out of these clothes, then," Alex said. She undressed Maggie unhurriedly. She acted calm and contained while Maggie's hormones raged. She needed Alex and needed her then. She took Alex's clothes off her, and they lay naked on the bed.

"I love the feel of your skin against mine," Maggie said. "It turns me on so much."

"Good. I love the feel of your skin period. I can't get enough of you."

She ran her hand over the length of Maggie's body. Maggie squirmed at her touch.

"Please," Maggie said. "Please don't tease me."

"I don't mean to tease you. I just love your body. I love the feel of it under my hand. I love how your skin ripples when I drag my hand over it."

She moved her hand over Maggie's breast and closed it over her nipple. Maggie felt her nipple stiffen at Alex's touch. Alex tugged and twisted at her nipple before replacing her hand with her mouth. Her warm moist breath on Maggie's nipple was almost too much for Maggie to stand. She shivered as her arousal heightened.

"Please," she begged again. "Please take me."

Alex released her nipple and kissed down her stomach. She positioned herself between her legs and kissed her softly. She sucked Maggie's lips between her own and ran her tongue between them. She buried her tongue deep inside Maggie before she moved it to her swollen clit. She sucked and licked at it until Maggie cried out as the orgasms cascaded over her.

When Maggie opened her eyes, Alex was smiling at her.

"That was amazing," Alex said.

"Yeah, it was. And now it's your turn."

"You can wait a minute, you know, get your strength back."

"Oh, it's back," Maggie said. "Trust me on that."

Maggie kissed Alex and tasted her own orgasms on her lips. She thought how good she tasted but knew it was nothing compared to the musky sweet flavor of Alex. She kissed down Alex and took one of her nipples in her mouth. She sucked it and felt it grow in her mouth. She ran her tongue around her areola and felt the small bumps there. She knew Alex was ready for her. And she was certainly ready for Alex.

She kissed lower and finally came to the heaven that was Alex. She ran her tongue over her and in her, thrusting her tongue as deep as it would go. She lapped at her walls and stroked them with her tongue. She ran her tongue all over her again and finally settled on her clit. She flicked it with her tongue over and over until Alex screamed her name as she climaxed.

Chapter Ten

Maggie woke the next morning in an empty bed. She rolled over and saw Alex packing their suitcases.

"Hey, gorgeous," Maggie said.

"Hey, beautiful. How'd you sleep?"

"Like a rock. Thanks to you." Maggie grinned.

"Mm." Alex came over and kissed Maggie. "My pleasure."

Maggie looked at the clock.

"We need to get in the shower," she said. "It's almost time to meet everyone for breakfast."

"Get up, then, lazybones."

"I'm up. I'm up."

Maggie made her way to the bathroom and turned on the shower. When it was warm enough, they climbed in.

"No funny business this morning," Maggie said. "We're running too late."

"Oh, man. Are you serious?"

"I am. We'll have to abstain until we're at our hotel tonight."

"That might kill me, but I'll do my best."

They dried off, dressed, and checked their room to make sure they hadn't left anything. Satisfied they hadn't, they grabbed their suitcases and went down to the dining room for a final meal in Rome.

They enjoyed their breakfast then climbed aboard the tour bus that would take them to their next stop, Orvieto. It was a short drive and Maggie enjoyed the countryside they passed on their way.

"It's all so Italian," she said.

Alex laughed.

"That it is."

They stopped in the center of town, on the Piazza del Duomo. They wandered through shops and bought some souvenirs before they made their way to the Gothic cathedral. The façade was magnificent. They stood admiring it for some time. The bas-relief on it was breathtaking. They stepped inside and observed the architecture and art inside. It was beautiful. Maggie walked determinedly to the Chapel of the Corporal, where there was supposedly a piece of cloth that had once bled. The blood spots formed a profile of Christ's face. Maggie wanted to see this. Alex followed just behind her. Maggie appreciated the space and nearness at the same time. She had no idea how she'd react to the cloth. The chapel was closed off by a wrought iron gate, precluding her from entering.

The center of the chapel contained a shrine that held the corporal. Maggie could just see the corporal through the translucent enamel part of the shrine. She struggled to maintain her footing. She wanted to collapse. She was so close to a miracle. It was enough to take her breath away.

"Are you okay?" Alex said. "You're shaking."

"I'm overwhelmed. The bloody corporal is right there."

"I see it. It's amazing, but I'm worried about you. Maybe we should get out of here."

"In a minute. I'll be ready in a minute."

Alex stood right next to her, lest she needed her support. True to her word, a moment or two later, Maggie turned.

"Okay. We can go."

They walked back out into the heat of the day. Maggie took a deep breath and inhaled the scents of the living. She couldn't forget the corporal. She never would, but she needed to move past it and enjoy what else Orvieto had to offer.

"There's the bakery over there that was recommended to us," Alex said. "It's been in business over a hundred years. You want to go check it out?"

"I'd love to." Maggie's stomach grumbled. "I'm famished."

They stepped inside the small café and found a table. The place smelled of decadence. The scents of chocolate and pastries wafted on the air.

"I'd love a pastry," Maggie said, "but I need something more substantial."

"Maybe we should each get a salad. We can have pastries for dessert."

"Excellent idea."

They enjoyed their salads and their decadent pastries.

"That was delicious," Maggie said.

"It was. Now, we need to get back on the bus. We don't want to keep them waiting."

Fortunately, they weren't the last ones back on the bus, which made Maggie feel good. Finally, everyone was on, and they took off for Assisi. They arrived at Grand Hotel Dei Congressi Assisi and went inside to put their bags away. They were to meet in one hour out front to get on the bus and go to the day's sightseeing locations.

"How are you feeling?" Alex pulled Maggie into her arms.

"I'm feeling good." Maggie was torn. She cared about Alex, and now that she was in her arms, she wanted her. But she felt guilty. She felt so in touch with her sisterhood that day. After seeing the corporal, she remembered why she was a nun. And being with Alex complicated that.

"You sure? You seem kind of distant."

"I'm not. I'm present with you."

"Okay. I'll take your word for it."

Alex ran her hands up and down Maggie's arms, and Maggie felt the fire flare deep within her. It betrayed her desire to keep her vows. She couldn't disregard it. She needed Alex. There was no denying that.

Maggie looked into Alex's eyes and saw a desire that matched her own. Alex lowered her head and claimed Maggie's lips with her own. Maggie kissed her back and opened her mouth to welcome her tongue. They stood kissing for what seemed an eternity. Finally, Maggie broke the kiss.

"Take me, Alex. Take me now."

Alex quickly undressed then stripped Maggie of her clothes. She took Maggie to bed and made love to her fiercely and passionately. She kissed her hard and moved her hand over her body with persistence. She seemed to need Maggie as much as Maggie needed her. She moved her hand between Maggie's legs and slipped her fingers inside her. She thrust them deeper and deeper as she urged Maggie to come.

Maggie arched off the bed, meeting each thrust. She moved against Alex's fingers until she arched, froze, and felt the orgasms wash over her. She collapsed back onto the bed and fought to catch her breath.

"That might have been the best yet," Maggie said.

"Really? Well, thank you."

"Mm. Now it's time for me to return the favor."

She skimmed her hand down Alex's body to where her legs met. Alex spread her legs and Maggie dipped her fingers inside. She stroked all along Alex's walls. Alex moved on the bed and groaned, encouraging her. Maggie found the soft spot that drove Alex mad and rubbed it enthusiastically. Alex cried out Maggie's name as she came.

They dressed hurriedly and got downstairs to get on the tour bus. The bus took them to Saint Clare's Church.

"The program says Saint Clare was a protégé of Saint Francis of Assisi," Alex said.

"That's way cool."

They entered the Gothic style church with the pink and white façade with the rest of the tour. The tour went down to the crypt where they saw the preserved body of Saint Clare. They made their way through the church and stopped to look at various artifacts.

"What a wonderful place," Maggie said. She was once again feeling her Catholicism strongly.

"Yeah. It was pretty impressive."

"I can't get over everything we've seen so far," Maggie said. "Thank you so much for bringing me on this trip."

"No problem. I wouldn't have missed it."

The next stop on the tour was Saint Francis's Basilica. It was considered to be the headquarters of the Franciscan Order, the Order to which Maggie belonged. She considered herself beyond blessed to be there.

While the others milled about, Maggie took her place in a pew and knelt to pray. Alex sat quietly next to her. Maggie lost herself in her prayers, thanking God for the opportunity to be there, thanking Him for calling her to serve. And she asked Him for guidance where Alex was concerned. She promised if He helped her, she would do what was right.

The tour was heading downstairs to the crypt that held Saint Francis's remains. Alex shook Maggie's shoulders. Maggie looked up, disoriented.

"They're going downstairs now. I thought you'd want to go," Alex said.

"Oh, yes. Definitely."

They followed the others downstairs, and Maggie felt a warm sensation of belonging wash over her as she looked at her founder's remains.

It was late afternoon when they left and headed back to the hotel.

"So, you want to get some dinner?" Alex said.

"Yes, please. I'd love that."

They each had delicious pasta dinners with wonderful salads. They split a chocolate cake for dessert.

"Oh, my God," Maggie said. "I'm so full."

"Me, too. Come on, let's go up to our room and work off this dinner."

Maggie was overcome with guilt. She wasn't sure she should make love with Alex, but she was so attracted to her. She wanted her. She couldn't deny it. She vowed to relax and enjoy her trip and time with Alex and worry about her vows when she got home.

"You okay?" Alex said as they entered the elevator.

"I'm fine. Why?"

"Sometimes you just disappear inside your head, and I want to make sure you're okay and we're okay."

"We're fine," Maggie said. "We're just fine."

"Good."

They arrived at their room, and Alex took Maggie in her arms.

"I'm crazy about you, woman," she said.

"I'm nuts about you, too."

"The past few days have been heaven. I love spending every moment with you."

"It has been wonderful," Maggie said.

"I wonder sometimes if you have second thoughts."

Maggie was silent. She should be honest. She knew it. But how to put it?

"I question what I'm doing sometimes," she said. "I took my vows years ago, and while I've broken them on occasion, I didn't break them knowingly and willingly several times a day. Sometimes I question what I'm doing. I have to be honest with you here. But I can't stay away from you. I want you. I need you. I crave you. And that doesn't seem to be changing any time soon."

Alex backed away slowly.

"I'm sorry to complicate your life," she said.

Maggie moved toward her and wrapped her arms around her neck.

"Please," she said. "Please don't do that. Not now. Let's enjoy this trip together. It's a special time for us. Please don't back away from me. Never move away from me. Always move toward me. I love your arms around me. I love it when you hold me and kiss me. Please don't deny me that."

"If you're sure, Mags. Promise me you're okay with it."

"I am. I need you, Alex. Please. Let's go to bed."

"Gladly."

She bent and kissed Maggie full on her lips. She continued to kiss her as she walked her over to the bed. She eased her down on it and climbed on top of her. She ground into her as they kissed.

She moved her knee up to Maggie's center and pressed into her. She could feel Maggie's wet heat through her shorts.

Alex moved her knee and unbuttoned and unzipped Maggie's shorts. She slid her hand inside them and under her underwear. Her hurried need for her made Maggie lightheaded with lust.

Alex slid her fingers inside Maggie and Maggie wriggled on them. She felt so good deep inside her. She moved around, urging Alex to touch all her sensitive spots. Alex moved in and out of her. She felt amazing. Maggie felt her nerves tense up in the pit of her stomach. She knew she was close. She continued to buck against Alex as she moved in and out. The nerves clenched tighter. She needed release desperately Soon the nerves unwound and white heat shot through her limbs as one climax after another rocked her body and soul.

"Oh, my God," Maggie breathed. "That was intense."

"I had to have you. I'm sorry I didn't even let you get naked."

"No. It was hot. Don't apologize. But now I want to get naked so I can have at you."

They stripped and fell back into bed together.

Maggie kissed down Alex's body until she arrived between her legs. She inhaled deeply, enjoying the scent that was all Alex. She bent to taste her, savoring her flavor. She moved her tongue deep inside her, stretching her tongue to its limits as she tried to lick deeper. She lapped at her walls as long as she could before she moved to her clit. It was swollen and slippery when she took it in her mouth and sucked on it. She flicked her tongue over it until Alex cried out her name.

They fell asleep in each other's arms. Maggie awoke first, and the sight of Alex's naked form lying beside her was too much to resist. She ran her hand down Alex's body and played her fingers between her legs. She coaxed the wetness out of Alex so she could easily enter her.

Alex woke up as Maggie pleased her deep inside.

"You feel so good," Alex said.

"Oh, you're awake. Good."

"How could I sleep through that?"

"I'm glad you feel that way."

Maggie continued to move in and out and listened carefully to Alex's moans urging her on. Maggie plunged her fingers as deep as they could go and Alex arched off the bed as she met every thrust. Maggie loved the feel of Alex moving against her. It spurred her onward. She finally found the spot she knew would send Alex over the edge. She rubbed at it slowly at first, then faster as Alex's breathing became more rapid. Finally, Alex let out a guttural moan, and Maggie knew she'd done a good job.

"You make me feel amazing," Alex said.

"I'm glad. I saw you lying there and couldn't resist."

"I'm glad. And now it's my turn."

Alex moved down Maggie's body and took one of her nipples in her mouth. She sucked and licked it until Maggie was gyrating on the bed. Alex kissed lower until she positioned herself between her legs. Maggie spread wide to allow her greater access.

Alex sucked and licked all over Maggie until Maggie cried out as she came.

"Shower time now," Alex said.

"Yeah. I suppose we should get ready for breakfast."

"Indeed. I'm starving."

They took a shower together, where Alex made Maggie climax several more times.

After, they dried off and dressed. They checked to make sure they hadn't left anything in the room and headed downstairs to meet the tour for another exciting day.

Chapter Eleven

The trip from Assisi to Florence was only about two and a half hours. Maggie was silent through much of the drive as she reflected on her feelings. She was beginning to admit to herself that she was falling in love with Alex. Or, rather, that she had fallen in love with her. She couldn't pinpoint exactly when it had happened, but it had. Should she tell Alex? Or would that only complicate things further? Besides, Alex was a reformed player. How would she react to hearing Maggie was in love with her? It might scare her away.

"Penny for your thoughts," Alex said.

"Oh, they're not worth a penny."

"You sure?"

"I'm sure."

"Is there anything you want to talk about?" Alex said.

Maggie reached out and squeezed her hand.

"No. I'm fine. Honest."

"Okay, but if you change your mind, I'm all ears."

"I appreciate that, Alex. I appreciate you more than you could possibly know."

Alex searched Maggie's eyes.

"Thank you. I appreciate you, too."

The bus pulled into Florence and dropped them off at the Academy of Fine Arts. They all got off the bus and milled around the obelisk in front of it as they waited for Teresa to lead them.

When everyone was off the bus, Teresa guided them all inside the building.

They walked through and admired the works of art, but Maggie was waiting for the next step in the tour. When Teresa finally announced they were going to the adjacent Gallery of the Academy of Florence, Maggie's stomach did somersaults. She couldn't believe she was finally going to see Michelangelo's *David*. She took several pictures of the famous statue and stood staring at it for quite a while.

"You sure seem to enjoy looking at a naked man," Alex teased her.

"It's *David*. It's famous, silly."

"I know. I know. I just didn't realize you'd be that into it."

"I am. Oh, my God, the talent Michelangelo had is awe-inspiring."

"This is true."

Their next stop was Giotto's Bell Tower, just one of the buildings that made up the Florence Cathedral. They marveled at the early Florentine Gothic architecture.

"It's gorgeous," Maggie said as she stared up at it.

"It really is."

"I can't get over all the architecture we've seen here."

"Neither can I. I'm loving this tour. I'm so glad we came."

"So am I. Oh, Alex, thank you again for bringing me."

"There's no one else I'd rather be with," Alex said.

Maggie blushed as she realized how much Alex cared for her. She might not be in love with her, but she certainly cared deeply for her.

"There are seven bells in there," Maggie read from their program. "I'd love to hear them ring."

Across from the Florence Cathedral, they arrived at the Florence Baptistery. The east doors of the Baptistery were designed by Michelangelo and dubbed the Gates of Paradise.

"Oh, my God. It's beautiful," Maggie said. "I don't think I'll ever recover from the beauty of this trip."

"Good. I want it embedded in your mind forever."

Their next stop was Signora Square, the focal point of the origin and of the history of the Florentine Republic. It was still the political hub of the city. They admired the multitude of sculptures as they wandered through the square.

"The amount of talent that sprung from this area blows the mind," Maggie said.

"No doubt. They did really good work back in the day."

Teresa blew a whistle, and they turned to see her holding up their tour sign. It was time to go.

"I don't want to leave," Maggie said. "I could stay in Florence for days."

"Ah, yes, but there's still so much to see."

"Yes, there is. Come on. Let's get on the bus."

Maggie enjoyed the scenery as they continued through the Apennine Mountains. The next thing Teresa told them was that they were in the flat area of Po. It was all beautiful to Maggie.

Finally, they arrived in Padua, where they would be staying the night at the Milano.

"Welcome to Padua," Teresa said. "Otherwise known as Saint Anthony's city. Saint Anthony of Padua is one of the Catholic Church's favorite saints. He is the patron saint of lost and stolen articles. You'll be on your own to look about the city. Enjoy."

She got off the bus, and the rest of them followed her. Maggie and Alex checked into their room and set their suitcases down. Alex moved to take Maggie in her arms.

"I'm so glad you're enjoying yourself," she said.

"You have no idea. And now we're in Padua. Did you know Saint Anthony was a Franciscan? I can't wait to see his church."

"Do you want to do that now? Or would you rather lie down for a bit?" Alex grinned.

"We should check out the church before it gets too late. Never fear, there'll be plenty of time for loving later."

"Okay."

"I'm sorry, Alex. Are you terribly disappointed?"

"No. No, really. I'm fine. This trip is for you and you said I could have you later. I'm going to hold you to that."

"Have I ever denied you before?"

"No."

"Okay, then," Maggie said. "Let's get going."

They took a taxi to the church. It was a minor basilica, according to their tour guide.

"It's huge," Maggie said. "Look at how beautiful it is."

"It's breathtaking," Alex said. "Let's go inside."

They entered the church and crossed themselves with holy water. They marveled at the frescoes then knelt to pray. Maggie felt an overwhelming sense of calm as she prayed, as was the norm for her. She got up, and Alex joined her. They wandered throughout the church some more, then walked out into the hot Italian night.

They hailed a taxi and went back to the hotel.

"You hungry, Mags?" Alex said.

"I'm starving. Let's eat before we go up to our room."

"Sounds good. I'm famished."

They enjoyed local Italian fare and after, shared tiramisu. After dinner, they made their way to their room. Once the door closed behind them, Alex pulled Maggie to her.

"You promised," she said.

"I did. And I plan to deliver."

Alex kissed Maggie hard on her mouth, her tongue prying her lips open to gain entry. Maggie welcomed Alex in and ran her tongue over hers. The sensations the kiss created left her craving more. She felt electricity coursing through her body as her need deepened. She pulled away and took Alex's hand. She led her to the bed.

Maggie stripped out of her clothes.

"Your turn," she said.

Alex quickly undressed and stood naked for Maggie's inspection.

"Your body takes my breath away," Maggie said.

"As does yours. Come on. Let's lie down. I need to have you."

They lay on the bed, and with no pretense, Alex climbed between Maggie's legs. She licked and sucked everything her mouth came in contact with. She coaxed one climax after another out of Maggie.

When she'd had her fill, Alex moved up next to Maggie and wrapped her arms around her.

"What do you think you're doing?" Maggie said.

"Holding you. What does it look like?"

"But I haven't had my way with you yet. Don't get so comfortable."

Maggie smiled into Alex's eyes as she skimmed her hand over her body. Her smile broadened as she reached between her legs and found her wet and ready for her.

"You feel amazing," Maggie said. She dipped her fingers inside Alex and stroked her satin walls. "You're so soft and silky inside."

"You feel amazing, too, Mags. Please. I need more."

Maggie slipped another finger inside and twisted her hand as she pulled it out and slid it back in.

"Holy shit, you feel good," Alex said.

"Oh, yeah. You want to come for me?"

"Hell, yes. Please, Maggie. Please get me off."

Maggie moved her fingers deeper inside Alex and moved them in and out faster and faster until Alex reached down, grabbed her wrist, and screamed as she came again and again. Maggie waited until the spasms had stopped before she came out of Alex. When she finally did, she settled into her arms and fell asleep.

They awoke early the next morning, excited to go to Venice.

"Today's going to be the best day yet. I can feel it," Maggie said.

"You're really excited to see Venice, aren't you?"

"Totally. Come on. Let's get showered so we can go downstairs and meet the group."

They took a long, hot shower. They lathered each other up, and Alex slid her fingers inside Maggie. Maggie fought to maintain her balance as the orgasms racked her body. Maggie slipped to her knees and buried her face between Alex's legs. Alex held on to Maggie's shoulders as she climaxed over and over.

After their shower, they toweled off and got dressed. They took their suitcases downstairs and joined the tour for breakfast. When breakfast was over, they climbed on the bus for the short drive to Venice.

Once there, they boarded a private boat and entered in style. Teresa joined up with another woman, Adriana, who would be their tour guide for the day. Maggie was shaking in anticipation when they arrived at Saint Mark's Square.

"Look at the basilica," she said.

"It's gorgeous."

"It's Italo-Byzantine architecture according to the program."

"Well, whatever it is, it's impressive."

Adriana led them across the square to the church. They passed under the four horses and entered. The high vaulted ceilings were similar to the other cathedrals they'd seen throughout Italy.

Maggie and Alex crossed themselves with holy water as they entered. Several others from the tour did the same. They wandered throughout the church, seeing as much as they could.

"The gold ground mosaics are amazing," Maggie said.

"No doubt. No wonder this place is also known as the church of gold."

They finally excused themselves from the group and knelt in front of the altar to pray. When they finished, the group was ready to head back outside. Their next stop was the Doge's Palace, the seat of government in Venice for centuries.

"More beautiful Gothic architecture," Maggie said.

"I love all the buildings we've seen on our tour."

"Me, too."

They took in the façade which overlooked the lagoon.

"Look at those sculptures," Maggie said.

"You and your sculptures." Alex reached an arm around Maggie and pulled her close. She held her for only a moment then let her go. But it was enough to suffuse Maggie in her warmth.

They wandered to the courtyard where Maggie immediately fell in love with the statues of Neptune and Mars. She took picture after picture. She wanted to remember everything forever.

Next up on the agenda was the Bridge of Sighs. They walked through the corridor to the prison.

"It says here this was named because prisoners walked this corridor and caught their final glimpse of the lagoon and the outside world before they were placed in their cells to serve their time," Maggie said.

"That makes sense. I'd breathe a heavy sigh, too, if I were them."

Their final stop on the tour was to watch a traditional glassblower. His work was on display, and Alex bought an orange vase.

"I've never seen flowers in your house," Maggie said.

"No. I'm just buying it for decoration, not for practicality."

"Got it."

The little shop was hot, and Alex and Maggie stepped out into the afternoon heat, which was less oppressive. The tour was over, and they wandered through small shops, and Maggie bought some souvenirs. Then it was time to catch the boat to Burano.

The island was as charming as it had been advertised. They disembarked and found themselves on a green.

"Look at that sculpture," Maggie said.

"This booklet says it's by Remigio Barbaro. I've never heard of him."

"Neither have I."

As they continued on, they admired the multicolored houses, ranging from pastel to vibrant pink. They made their way to the center of the island to Galuppi Square. They saw many old ladies working their lace.

"I guess this place is known for its lace," Maggie said.

"Well, there are plenty of shops that sell it." Alex looked around. "Are you interested?"

"Not particularly. I'll tell you what, I'm hungry. How about you?"

"Yeah. I could use some food."

They found a restaurant and ordered fresh fish plates. They weren't disappointed.

"That was delicious," Maggie said when they were through.

"It really was. Now, we'd better make our way back to the boat. I'd hate to miss it or the bus back to Padua."

They arrived in Venice just in time to board the bus.

"I'm glad we didn't have to leave without you," Teresa said as she boarded.

"Sorry," Maggie said.

"It's okay. You made it on time, but barely." She smiled at them.

Once back at Padua, they went to their room and sat on the bed.

"What a day," Maggie said. "It was truly amazing."

"Yes, it was. How about we keep the amazement going?"

She kissed Maggie. It was soft and sweet and left Maggie wanting more. Maggie wrapped her arms around Alex and pulled her close. She pressed her tongue to Alex's lips and pried them open. She snaked her tongue inside Alex's mouth and ran hers along the length of Alex's.

Alex was breathing heavily when the kiss broke. She stood and stripped then pulled Maggie up and undressed her. She eased her on the bed and Maggie lay back with her legs wide. Alex climbed between them and lapped greedily at the juices that flowed there. She buried her tongue as deep as it would go and ran it over her walls. She took her tongue out and licked Maggie's clit. Maggie pressed her face into her as she moved around on the bed, unable to lie still.

Finally, Maggie lay still as she felt the ball of energy coalesce deep in her center. She focused on Alex and the energy until the ball broke loose and shot waves of orgasms over her body.

"That was insane," she said when she'd caught her breath. "You are an amazing lover."

"Thanks. I'm glad you enjoyed it. I sure did."

"Did you now? How much?"

Maggie placed her hand between Alex's legs and felt how wet and ready she was.

"Oh, yeah," she said. "You did enjoy it."

"Yeah, I did."

Maggie slipped her fingers inside Alex then and stroked her as deep as she could get. She tickled everything deep inside with her fingertips. Alex moved on the bed, urging Maggie deeper. Maggie reached as far as she could then took her fingers out and ran them over Alex's clit.

Alex cried out as she convulsed with one climax after another.

"We need to get some sleep now," Alex said. "Tomorrow's another big day."

"Okay. Will you hold me, please?"

"Gladly. Nothing would make me happier."

Secure in Alex's arms, Maggie fell into a deep sleep.

Chapter Twelve

The first stop the next day on their tour was the city of Verona, the setting for Shakespeare's *Romeo and Juliet*. They took pictures of Juliet's balcony and rubbed the shining breast on her statue for good luck.

"I'll rub your breast for good luck any time," Alex whispered.

"You're so bad." She swatted Alex on the arm.

"Ah, but I'm also so good."

"Yes, you are," Maggie blushed.

Next, they went to the Arena, a well preserved pink Roman amphitheater.

"Oh, look at it," Maggie said. "It's so peaceful. It's hard to believe gladiators used to fight here."

"I hear ya. It's so much easier to see it as the opera venue it is today."

They all piled onto the bus for the drive to Milan. Teresa led them to La Scala Opera House. It was beautiful, and Maggie asked another tourist to take a picture of Alex and her in front of it.

After that, they went to the Galleria, one of the world's oldest shopping malls. The glass-domed ceilings let the sunlight shine on them as they made their way from one upscale store to another. They grabbed lunch at a restaurant that had been there since 1867. After lunch, they met the rest of the tour out front for their next stop, which was the Milan Cathedral.

"The pamphlet says it took six centuries to build this bad boy," Alex said. "It's the fifth largest church in the world."

"I'd believe that. It's incredibly huge."

"And it's more of that Gothic architecture we love so much."

"And look at those gargoyles. I love gargoyles."

"Really? They're kind of grotesque."

"I think they're awesome."

"Okay, then."

They walked into the cathedral and were in awe of the magnificent artwork inside. As was the norm now, they knelt in front of the altar and prayed for a few moments. Maggie had the familiar sense of peace as she rose to her feet. Alex joined her.

They rejoined the group and wandered through the exquisite church. They were blown away by everything they saw.

"This place is magnificent," Maggie said.

"It's beyond magnificent."

"Yeah, I suppose it is."

After their tour of the cathedral, the bus took them to the hotel. Maggie and Alex found their room and collapsed on the bed.

"I don't know the last time I did this much walking," Maggie said.

"It's good for us."

"Oh, I know. It's just that it's catching up with me now."

"Did you want to nap before dinner?" Alex said.

"I don't think I need a nap, per se. I just need to be off my feet for a while."

"Oh, good." Alex grinned. "I know just the thing to take your mind off your feet."

"You do, huh?"

"Yes, I do."

Alex rolled over on top of Maggie and kissed her hard on her mouth. Maggie responded with a passionate kiss of her own. They kissed for what seemed like hours, but in reality was only a few minutes. Maggie pulled away breathless.

"That was some kiss," she said.

"Its purpose was to get your juices flowing."

Maggie felt the moisture pooling between her legs.

"It definitely worked."

"Did it?" Alex said. "Let me see."

She unbuttoned and unzipped Maggie's shorts. She slid her hand inside her underwear and found Maggie wet and swollen for her.

"You feel so good," she said.

"Please, Alex. Please don't tease me."

"Ah, but teasing can be so much fun." She dragged her fingers over the length of Maggie.

"But not now. Please. I need you."

Alex positioned her hand so that her fingers moved easily inside Maggie. They groaned together.

"That feels amazing," Maggie said. "Please go deeper."

Alex thrust her fingers in as deep as they would go. Maggie arched off the bed, meeting each thrust and urging Alex onward. She felt herself grow tight inside and focused only on Alex. The tension inside her let loose and shot white-hot chills all over her body as she came.

Maggie fumbled with Alex's shorts. She finally got them off and slid her underwear down her legs and off as well. She climbed between Alex's legs. As always, she took a moment to admire Alex's beauty before she lowered her face and tasted her.

"You're delicious," she said.

"Thank you. Now it's my turn to beg you not to tease me. I need you, Mags. I need you so bad."

Maggie licked all over Alex and felt her squirm on the bed. She quit teasing her and buried her tongue as deep as it would go. She strained it trying to lick deeper and finally relaxed it and lapped at the soft spot that Alex favored. She ran her tongue over it several times before Alex cried out as she reached her climax.

They dozed together for a little while and woke famished.

"Let's go get some dinner," Alex said.

"Sounds good to me. But let's not eat in the hotel. Let's go to a restaurant in the city."

"Ah. An adventure. Sounds good to me."

They took a shower where they enjoyed each other's body at length. They got out, dried off, and dressed for dinner.

"Let's ask the concierge where she recommends," Maggie said.

"Excellent idea."

They arrived at the front desk and posed the question to the concierge.

"Do you like wine?" she said.

"We love wine," Maggie said.

"For something different, may I suggest Boccondivino? They bring you different wines paired with different foods. It's not like you get a meal, per se, but you certainly get enough to eat. Does that interest you?"

"That sounds different," Alex said. They looked at each other. Maggie nodded.

"I think we'll try it."

"It should be quiet still at seven thirty. You should be okay to get seated. I'll hail you a taxi."

"That won't be necessary. We'll find one. Thank you, though," Alex said.

They stepped out into the warm night air, and Alex hailed a cab. They arrived at the restaurant in no time. They were greeted immediately and given their choice of a communal table or a private one. They chose the private table and were seated at one in the middle of the restaurant.

A handsome waiter approached their table.

"I'm Vincenzo," he said. "I'll be your waiter and guide to your food and wine experience. To get you started, may I ask what your favorite wine is?"

"Malbec," Alex said.

"Ah, excellent choice. I will pair your dishes with smooth red wines then."

"Oh, thank you."

They were served seven courses, including vegetables and antipasto, various cheeses and salami, and finally biscotti for dessert. Each course was paired with a different wine. By the end of the meal, Maggie and Alex were both satiated and buzzed. Maggie caught the giggles and asked for a cup of coffee in an attempt to sober up. Alex just sat there watching Maggie with a look of lust in her eyes.

Maggie blushed under the scrutiny, but deep down, she loved it. She loved how into her Alex was. She also loved knowing what was in store for her when she got back to the hotel.

Alex paid the bill, and they hailed another taxi to the hotel. Once in their room, they quickly stripped and fell into bed together. Alex kissed Maggie all over. She kissed her lips, her cheeks, her forehead, and her eyelids. It seemed like she couldn't get enough of her.

She kissed down Maggie's body, stopping to suckle at a nipple. She tugged it with her lips and ran her tongue over it. Maggie was writhing on the bed under her. She kissed lower and positioned herself between Maggie's legs. Maggie spread herself wide for Alex.

Alex lapped at Maggie's lips. She sucked them and ran her tongue between them. Then she buried her tongue deep inside Maggie before moving it to her swollen clit. She took it in her mouth and sucked on it as she flicked it with the tip of her tongue. Maggie pressed Alex's face into her as she moved against her. Around and around, she gyrated her hips as she made Alex fight to keep her tongue on her clit. Finally, Maggie quit moving. She was perfectly still as she screamed Alex's name. She collapsed on the bed, spent.

"That was indescribable," Maggie said.

"I'm glad you enjoyed it. I sure did."

Maggie kissed Alex then, a passionate kiss that left her breathless. She moved her hand down between her legs and felt how wet and ready Alex was for her. She slipped her fingers inside as deep as they would go. She wriggled her fingertips in an effort to touch everything inside. Alex grabbed her wrist and guided her hand in and out. Maggie let Alex do what she needed to do. She was simply the conduit. Alex was in control. Alex moved her hand in and out over and over and finally froze as she issued a guttural moan and climaxed on Maggie's hand.

They fell asleep with their limbs entwined and awoke the next morning to pick up where they left off. Alex skimmed her hand over

Maggie's body until it came to rest between her legs. She moved her fingers in and out of Maggie until Maggie's breathing came in gasps. Alex slid her fingers out and pressed them into Maggie's clit. Maggie saw stars as she rode wave after wave of orgasm.

Maggie kissed down Alex's body until she was between her legs. She licked and sucked everything she found. Alex pressed her face into her. Maggie could barely breathe but kept going until Alex cried out as the orgasms washed over her.

They got in the shower together, and this time it was Alex who dropped to her knees and buried her face between Maggie's legs. She played her tongue over her until Maggie dug her fingers into Alex's shoulders to keep from falling as she climaxed.

Maggie rubbed Alex between her legs until Alex rewarded her with a scream as she came.

They dried off, dressed, and went downstairs to meet their group for the last full day of the tour. The last day consisted of a boat ride to beautiful Lake Como. They went to the city of Bellagio, situated on the lake with a view of the Alps behind it. It was beautiful, and the tour wandered through the city, then they were released on their own in the Borgo to shop and eat. Alex and Maggie made their way to the Basilica of San Giacomo. It was dark and cool inside, but they still enjoyed it. They knelt in front of the ornate altar and prayed before wandering through it again. They admired the frescoes and the sculptures before walking out into the warm midday sun.

They went back to the center of town and had toc, a traditional dish from the area. It had polenta and butter and cheese. Alex had dried fish with hers and Maggie had homemade salami. They shared a jug of red wine and afterward, enjoyed miascia for dessert. They were pleasantly full and somewhat buzzed. They shopped for a little while before it was time to get on the boat and head back to Milan.

Once back, they went to their room and made love before dinner.

"It seems all we've done on this vacation is eat," Maggie said.

"Speaking of eating."

Alex slid between her legs and devoured her. Maggie screamed as she came one time after another.

Maggie returned the favor, and they lay on the bed, satisfied and content.

"What time is dinner?"

"It's in an hour. We have time for a shower."

"Most excellent." Maggie grinned.

They got into the shower and lathered each other up. Maggie spent extra time scrubbing Alex between her legs. She played her fingers over her and rubbed her soapy clit until Alex's knees buckled as she came.

Alex ran her hands over Maggie's body. She stopped to pinch her nipples. She tweaked one then the other. She moved her hand lower and delved deep inside Maggie. Maggie fought for balance as the orgasms racked her body. Once clean and dry, they dressed for dinner and went downstairs to catch the bus.

The bus took them to Calafuria Unione where they dined on risotto and drank wine with the rest of their tour mates. It was a melancholy occasion. They all enjoyed their final dinner together but were sad that the tour was coming to an end.

After dinner, Alex asked Teresa about women's clubs in Milan.

"There are plenty of clubs that are listed as gay friendly, but I don't know any that cater specifically to women. I would suggest the Ginger Cocktail Lab. They have great drinks and a wonderful atmosphere. And I don't think you'll stick out like a sore thumb if that's what you're worried about."

"That sounds good. We'll check it out."

They hailed a cab and arrived shortly at the bar. The ambiance was great, and they took seats at the bar. The bartender patiently explained their specialty drinks. Maggie ordered a honey fizz while Alex opted for the bison mojito. They were both happy with their drinks and ordered several more. The place had a decent crowd, but not so much so that they couldn't talk quietly at their places.

The music that was playing was a mix of contemporary and nineties rock. They enjoyed themselves immensely, and it was late when they finally poured themselves into a taxi to return to the hotel.

Once in their rooms, they hurriedly undressed each other and fell into bed again.

"I swear, I can't get enough of you," Alex said.

"That's a good thing. There's plenty more of me for you to have."

"Excellent answer."

Alex thrust her fingers deep inside Maggie and stroked her until she climaxed all over her hand.

Maggie climbed between Alex's legs.

"What a perfect dessert for the night," she said. She buried her tongue inside her and lapped as deep as she could. She moved her tongue to Alex's clit. Alex exploded in her mouth, and Maggie licked up the juices before moving up to kiss Alex.

"Damn, I taste good," Alex said.

"That you do, my love. That you do."

"What did you call me?"

"Huh? What?"

"You called me your love. Did you mean that?"

Maggie was unsure how to respond.

"I don't know," she said. "Maybe it was just a term of endearment."

"Maybe, but maybe not. So I'm asking you, Maggie. Do you love me?"

Maggie's stomach was in knots. She knew she loved Alex, but as a player, how would Alex react to such a declaration?

"Yes," she said. "I think I do."

Alex broke into a wide smile.

"That's awesome. Because I love you, too."

They made love again to celebrate and, finally exhausted, fell asleep wrapped in each other's arms.

Chapter Thirteen

Morning arrived, and they showered, dressed, grabbed their luggage, and went downstairs to meet the group for their final meal. Breakfast was fun. People were exchanging phone numbers and email addresses. Maggie and Alex hadn't connected with anybody like that. They met people, and they'd enjoyed their company, but they had been too into each other to get to know anyone that well. So they ate their breakfast and watched the goings-on of others.

When breakfast was over, they hugged Teresa and thanked her for a wonderful vacation. Alex tipped her handsomely then they went about their day. They stowed their luggage at the concierge's station so they could spend a few hours wandering through the city. Their flight left that afternoon, so they didn't have a lot of time.

"Where do you want to go? What do you want to see?" Alex said.

"I'd really like to go to the Holy Mary of Grace Monastery. I'd like to see Da Vinci's *Last Supper* as long as we're here."

"Sounds good to me."

They got in a taxi and arrived at the monastery. They went to the refectory of the convent and saw the painting. It was even more beautiful than Maggie had imagined. Her eyes watered as she looked at it. It was one of the holiest occasions in her Church caught with paint.

"You okay?" Alex said.

"I will be. I just get chills looking at it."

"Well, take as long as you need."

The crowds hadn't arrived yet, so Maggie took her time gazing at the mural.

As more people filed in, Alex touched Maggie's arm.

"Hey, more people are coming in now."

"Huh? Oh. Okay. We can go now."

They walked out into the afternoon air.

"We don't have time to see anything else," Alex said. "We need to get our bags and head to the airport."

"Sounds good to me. Oh, Alex. Thank you again so much for giving me this opportunity. It means the world to me."

"My pleasure. Anything for you, my love."

The sound of the words filled Maggie with joy. And then confusion. How could she love Alex and Christ? She didn't know, but she knew she did. She loved them both fiercely and hated the idea that she would someday have to choose between the two of them.

The flights back home were uneventful. They flew into LAX, had dinner, then caught their puddle jumper home. They spent the night at Alex's house where they made sweet love all night. They made the most of their last night together. They took turns pleasing each other until, exhausted, Maggie fell asleep in Alex's arms.

Late Saturday morning, Alex dropped Maggie off at the convent. Maggie was sad to say good-bye but took solace in the fact she would spend the next afternoon with Alex. She let herself into her room, where she found a note from Reverend Mother welcoming her home and asking her to stop by her office on Monday to show her pictures. Maggie smiled. She had plenty of pictures to share. That was for sure.

Maggie unpacked then dropped to her knees in front of her crucifix. She thanked God for her safe trip and for all she got to see and do. Then she asked God once again for guidance as far as Alex was concerned. She didn't know if He heard her or was ignoring her or if He just wanted her to work things out on her own because she didn't feel any different when she stood from her prayers.

She went to the dining room for dinner. Reverend Mother joined her.

"Hello, dear. Tell me. How was your trip?"

"It was fantastic, Reverend Mother. We saw so many wonderful things and so many fantastic cathedrals and churches. I got your note. I'll definitely show you the pictures Monday."

"Wonderful. I'm so glad you weren't disappointed."

"Not at all. In fact, it surpassed all my expectations."

"That's great to hear."

They finished their dinner and Maggie said good night. Jet lag had caught up with her big time. She fell asleep as soon as her head hit the pillow.

The following day, she showered and dressed for Mass. She was excited to see Alex. Even though she'd just seen her the day before and spent the week before with her, she missed her like crazy.

She sang the processional hymn loudly while she watched the door for Alex to walk in. When she did, her heart skipped a beat. She watched her genuflect and take her spot in the usual pew. She smiled broadly at her and Alex grinned back. Maggie told herself to get it together and focus on the Mass, which she did.

After Mass, they met at the coffee and doughnut social.

"How you doin'?" Alex said.

"I'm okay. How are you?"

"I've missed you."

"That's sweet, but I just saw you yesterday."

"So you haven't missed me, too?"

"I'd be a liar if I said that." Maggie smiled.

"Good. That's what I wanted to hear. Now, you go mingle. I'll hang around so we can go to my place later."

"Sounds good to me. Excuse me."

There weren't as many parishioners there as usual, as it was summer vacation and many of them were out of town. But there were enough to keep Maggie busy. Many asked about her trip, and she thrilled them with her stories of where she'd been and what she'd seen.

When the last parishioner had left, Maggie and Alex helped clean up, then they went by Maggie's room so she could change.

As soon as her door closed, Alex took Maggie in her arms.

"Careful," Maggie whispered. "These doors don't have locks."

"Bummer." Alex stepped away and slid her hands into her pants pockets. "I'll behave myself then."

"Thanks."

Maggie changed, and they walked out to the truck to head to Alex's house. Once out on the street, Alex took Maggie's hand.

"It's so good to see you. What am I going to do with the week ahead? I can't believe I have to go a whole week without seeing you."

"I know. It's going to be hard. But I'm out of school, so maybe we can get together a couple of afternoons."

"That would be great."

"Sure. Depending on what time you finish work."

"I'd love that," Alex said.

They arrived at the house and were in each other's arms before the door even closed.

"I love you, Maggie. I love you so much." She kissed Maggie passionately, and Maggie felt it to her core. She pulled away.

"I love you, too."

They walked upstairs to the bedroom and stripped each other of their clothes. They lay together naked and gazed at each other's bodies as if they'd never seen them before.

"You're so beautiful," Alex said.

"As are you."

"I have missed you so much. I was exhausted last night but had a hell of a time falling asleep because you weren't in my arms."

"Yeah. We kind of got spoiled on vacation," Maggie said.

"Yeah, we did."

"So, are we going to make up for not being together last night? Or are we just going to talk?"

"Oh, we're going to make up for not being together last night." Alex grinned.

She kissed Maggie again, and Maggie felt the moisture pool at her center. She was so ready for Alex to take her.

"I'm ready," she said. "Please."

Alex slid her hand between Maggie's legs and felt how ready she was. She slipped her fingers inside her and stroked her with her powerful fingers. Maggie arched off the bed, lost in the feelings Alex was creating. She couldn't think of anything but Alex's fingers, and soon she felt her world explode into a million tiny pieces as the orgasms crashed over her.

She finally came back to earth and lay there with her eyes closed, trying to catch her breath.

"Wow," she said. "That was something else."

"Yeah? Good."

"Good is an understatement."

Maggie ran her hand over Alex's tight body and brought it to rest between her legs. She slid her fingers inside her and rubbed her walls. She brought her fingers to Alex's clit and pressed into it. Alex cried out as she came.

They lay together for a few moments, simply enjoying being together again.

"Shall we go for a swim?" Alex said.

"Sounds good to me."

Maggie swam a few laps then took her place on the steps. She watched Alex finish her laps and swim over to join her.

"You look so beautiful sitting here," Alex said. She placed her hand on Maggie's thigh and slowly moved it up toward her center.

"I do, huh?"

"Yeah, you do." Her hand found Maggie's center, and she dipped her fingers inside her.

"Mm," Maggie said. "That feels nice."

"Yeah?" Alex kissed her and pressed their breasts together as she continued to move in and out of Maggie. In no time, Maggie buried her face in Alex's shoulder to keep from screaming out loud.

"You're amazing," Maggie said.

"Why's that?"

"You never stop. And I love that."

"I can't get enough of you," Alex said. "I need more and more of you every time I see you."

"That makes me so happy."

"Good. I always want to make you happy."

"I'm getting hungry," Maggie said. "Should we start making dinner?"

"I don't have a thing in the house. Maybe we should go out to get something? I know a great steakhouse."

"Sounds good to me."

They dried off in the sun and went inside to get dressed. Alex drove them to the other side of town to Tahoe Joe's. They each had juicy steaks with potatoes and vegetables.

"This is delicious," Maggie said. "Thank you so much for bringing me here."

"I can't believe you've never been here."

While they ate, some parishioners approached the table.

"Sister Mary Margaret?" the woman said. "We thought that was you."

"It is. Hello. How are you guys?

"We're great. How fun seeing you out on the town."

"Even nuns get dinner out once in a while."

Maggie introduced Alex to the family.

"Oh, yes," the woman said. "We've seen you at Mass. We've never even thought about asking a nun to dinner. I bet that would be a nice thing to do. We'll have to do that sometime."

"It's a wonderful gesture. That's for sure."

"Okay, well, we'll leave you to your dinner. It was good seeing you."

"Good seeing you, too. We'll see you Sunday."

"Definitely."

After they'd walked off, Alex grew serious.

"What's up?" Maggie said.

"Do you worry about being seen in public with me?"

"Why would I?"

"I kind of scream lesbian."

"But," Maggie said, "you are a Catholic. Those usually offset each other. So, no, I don't worry about what people would think."

"Well, I do. Maybe we shouldn't go out to eat anymore."

"Nonsense. I'm a big girl, Alex. If I want to be seen with you, I will. It's not like we're holding hands or fawning all over each other or anything like that. We're two women having dinner. Relax."

"I'll try."

They finished their dinner and walked to the truck. Once inside, Alex took Maggie's hand.

"I'm sorry I freaked out at dinner," she said.

"It's okay. I get where you're coming from, but I don't worry so neither should you."

"I never want to put you in a compromising position," Alex said.

"You don't?" Maggie smiled.

"Well, not in public."

Alex squeezed Maggie's hand, and they rode back to the convent in silence.

"So, when can I see you again?" Alex said as she cut the engine.

"I was thinking Tuesday. As much as I'd love to see you every day, I need to help out around the convent. I can meet you at three o'clock on Tuesday and we can go to your place for a couple of hours. I need to be home by six for dinner."

"Fair enough. I'll be here at three or shortly thereafter."

"Sounds wonderful. I'll see you then." Maggie moved to get out of the truck.

"I'll miss you," Alex said.

"I'll miss you, too."

Maggie got out and waved good-bye as Alex backed out. She let herself in the convent and ran into Reverend Mother.

"Hello, Maggie," she said.

"Hello, Reverend Mother."

"Maggie, may I have a moment with you?"

"Sure."

"Let's go to my office."

Maggie's stomach was in knots. What could Reverend Mother possibly want to talk to her about that couldn't wait until morning, when Maggie had already promised to come to her office to show her pictures of her trip?

"Maggie," Mother Superior said. "I'm worried about you."

"How so?"

"You've been spending a lot of time with that Alex Foster."

"Yes, I have. She's a wonderful person." Maggie was careful not to show any emotion.

"Well, she strikes me as very masculine."

"She seems to be."

"I don't want you getting into trouble, Maggie."

"What sort of trouble would I get into?" Maggie said.

"Maggie, do I need to remind you that you took vows of chastity, poverty, and obedience?"

Maggie's mouth went dry. This was not a conversation she wanted to have.

"No, ma'am. I don't need a reminder. I'm well aware of my vows."

"I just know that you just got back from a dream vacation that I'm sure cost Ms. Foster a pretty penny. I don't want you longing to live the good life now. Your vow of poverty is still in place."

"Yes, ma'am. I know that."

"I won't ask you about your vow of chastity. But I will remind you that that applies to men and women. I know Ms. Foster is a very handsome woman and you may be tempted, but I want you to maintain your vows."

"I will," Maggie lied. "I am always aware of my vows, Reverend Mother. I keep them in the forefront of everything I do."

"Very well. You're free to go to bed now. I'll see you in the morning to look at your pictures?"

"Yes, ma'am, you will."

"Great. Good night, Maggie."

"Good night, Reverend Mother."

Maggie went to her room and lay on her bed. Tears leaked from her eyes, slowly at first and soon she was sobbing. Reverend Mother knew. Or at least suspected. What was she going to do? She finally cried herself to sleep.

Chapter Fourteen

Monday morning, Maggie grabbed the digital camera Alex had given her and walked down the hall to Reverend Mother's office.

"Reverend Mother?" she said. "Is now a good time?"

"Of course, my child. Come on in."

Reverend Mother took a seat next to Maggie on one side of her desk. Maggie started from the beginning and scrolled through all the pictures she'd taken.

"Oh, wow," Reverend Mother said of her pictures of the Vatican. "I can't believe you were there."

"It was amazing."

"The obelisk," Reverend Mother said. "Where Saint Peter was crucified. I'm getting chills."

"Oh, Reverend Mother. It was the perfect vacation for a Catholic."

They continued looking at the pictures. Reverend Mother blushed a deep red when she saw the picture of David.

"Oh, my," she said. "I'm not so sure I needed to see that."

"Reverend Mother, it's a work of art. A famous one, at that. I think everyone should see it."

"If you say so, my dear. I still can't keep from blushing."

"And that's okay."

When they were through looking at the pictures, Maggie stood to leave.

"Maggie?"

"Yes?"

"Have you given any more thought to our conversation last night?"

"Don't worry, Reverend Mother," Maggie lied again. "My vows are firmly in place."

"I'm glad to hear that. That puts my mind at ease."

"Good. I'll see you later, Reverend Mother."

Maggie went to her room and put on some thrasher clothes. She planned to spend the day in the garden pulling weeds. She planned to just space out as she did this, but instead, her mind wouldn't shut off. She kept replaying her conversations with Reverend Mother. She wasn't concerned about her vow of poverty, but her vow of chastity had been shot all to hell. She knew she needed to make some hard choices, but wasn't ready. She wasn't ready to choose between Alex and her calling. She knew that, at the moment, she wasn't giving her all to either and that wasn't fair, but she wasn't ready to decide who would get her full, undivided attention.

She finished in the garden, and it was almost time for dinner. She went in and took a hot shower, letting the water pound her sore muscles. She dried off and went to the dining room. She got there just before Reverend Mother said grace.

Maggie enjoyed her dinner with the other nuns and engaged them all in stories of her trip. They all had questions and begged to see pictures. She promised them all she'd share with them. Everyone was suitably impressed. And Maggie loved reliving the wonderful vacation. She promised to show the group her pictures at lunch the next day.

When dinner was over, Maggie went back to her room. She dropped to her knees, ignoring the pain in them, and prayed. She thanked God for the wonderful experience she'd had on the trip and thanked Him for the sisters with whom she shared the convent. She once again asked Him for guidance where Alex was concerned, but when she was through praying, she didn't have any answers. Even though it was early, Maggie climbed into bed, exhausted.

She awoke the next morning and went to the dining room for breakfast. She made a waffle, had some yogurt, and poured a cup of coffee. She took a seat away from the others as she was still lost in her own head. She said grace and ate quietly, undisturbed.

After breakfast, she went out to the garden to do some more weeding. It gave her something to do until lunch. She took a shower, changed her clothes, and went to the dining room to meet the nuns who wanted to see her pictures.

They all gathered around, and Maggie lost herself once again in the pictures and in reliving her vacation. The nuns were suitably impressed and asked all sorts of questions. She answered them all to the best of her ability. They sat and talked and ate until two o'clock rolled around. The group slowly dispersed to go do their chores. Maggie felt she'd already put in enough time, so went to her room to await Alex's arrival.

At precisely three o'clock, she cut through the garden to the parking lot. There was Alex, looking gorgeous, even though she was filthy. Maggie climbed into the truck and fought the urge to lean over and kiss her.

"You look dashing," Maggie said.

"I'm a dirty mess."

"It becomes you."

"Thanks, I guess."

They arrived at Alex's house.

"I need a shower," Alex said. "Would you like to join me?"

"I'd love to."

They got in the shower and lathered each other up. Maggie washed Alex all over before slipping her fingers inside her to please her. She moved them in and out until Alex leaned against the wall of the shower, satiated.

Alex dropped to her knees and licked Maggie's clean center. She lapped at her juices and sucked her clit until Maggie dug her fingers into Alex and cried out as she came.

"That was a nice appetizer," Alex said. They dried off and lay on the king-sized bed.

"Just look at you," Maggie said. "I just love your body."

"I love everything about you."

"Well, there's that."

Alex kissed Maggie then. It was a deep, soul-searing kiss that made Maggie melt. She felt herself swell and get wet like only Alex could make her. She arched into Alex as the kiss continued, begging her with her actions.

Alex seemed to grasp what Maggie was doing. She climbed down her body until she was between her legs.

"You're beautiful," she said. "Just beautiful."

She lowered her head and took Maggie in her mouth. She licked and sucked on every inch of her, leaving no part untouched. She moved her mouth to Maggie's clit as she slid her fingers inside her. Maggie felt the orgasm building. She thrashed her head from side to side the closer it got. Finally, she felt the wonderful release as she climaxed several times.

When Alex was lying next to Maggie again, Maggie ran her hand down Alex's body, pausing when she reached her taut belly.

"You're so muscular. I love it."

"Thank you. It goes with the work I do."

"Well, I love it." She moved her hand lower and found Alex wet and ready for her. She slipped her fingers inside and thrust them as deep as they could go. She strained to reach all the inner parts of her with her fingertips. She loved the feel of Alex and loved pleasing her this way.

She finally slid her hand out and rubbed Alex's clit just like she liked it.

"Oh, God," Alex called. "Oh, dear God. Yes. Yes, that's it." She arched off the bed and froze as the orgasms washed over her.

Maggie climbed up next to her.

"You are so good at that," Alex said.

"Thanks. You let me know what you like, so it's pretty easy."

"Well, I'm sure glad I have you."

"Me, too."

They lay like that for a few minutes before Alex took Maggie again and again. Maggie lay exhausted.

"I've got no more," Maggie said. "I don't even think I have the energy to return the favor."

"That's okay. I need to get you home for dinner anyway. We can't have you being late."

Maggie thought of the conversations she'd recently had with Reverend Mother. She wondered if she should tell Alex about them but decided against it. She figured it was her cross to bear.

They drove back to the convent.

"When will I see you again?" Alex said.

"How about Thursday? Same time, same place?"

"Sounds good to me. I'll be counting the minutes until I see you again."

"You say the sweetest things."

"I say the truth."

"Thanks, Alex," Maggie said.

"My pleasure."

Maggie opened the truck door.

"I'll see you Thursday," Alex said.

"See you then."

She let herself in the convent and went straight to the dining room for dinner. After dinner, she helped in the kitchen just for something to do. When she was through there, she went to her room and prayed some more before falling into bed.

The next day was beautiful, and Maggie decided to walk through town and look at people. Lunch was not a required meal at the convent, so she grabbed a sandwich at Firestone's. It was delicious, and she washed it down with a couple of beers.

She wandered through town again, watching all the happy couples, some on vacation and some she recognized as locals. They all seemed so happy, and Maggie missed Alex so much it was painful. She wanted to walk through town holding her hand, but that couldn't be. Maggie was married to the Church. And she was happy to be, right? She pondered yet again the dilemma she had gotten herself into. She wished she had answers, but she didn't. And missing Alex wasn't helping.

Maggie went back to her room and dropped to her knees. She prayed harder than she'd ever prayed in her life, but still, she received no answers. Her knees hurt when she finally got off them and went to the dining room for dinner. There, surrounded by her sisters, she felt a sense of calm. She loved them and loved this life. But was there really room in this life for Alex? She hoped so, as she was so in love with her, she couldn't imagine giving her up.

Thursday afternoon finally arrived, and Maggie and Alex were alone in Alex's house.

"I need another shower. You joining me?"

"You'd better believe it."

They showered together and brought each other to several orgasms. After, they went out to the pool where they swam some laps. Maggie took her usual spot and watched Alex gracefully cut through the water. She had the most amazing body, and Maggie couldn't get enough of it.

This time, when Alex sat down, it was Maggie who took the initiative. She slid her fingers inside Alex and watched her eyes close in pleasure. Maggie continued what she was doing until Alex let out a guttural moan as she came.

"Let's get inside," Alex said. "I need you."

"But we're all wet."

"Fine, then, sit on this wall here."

Maggie climbed out of the pool and sat where she was directed. Her legs dangled in the pool, but she was the perfect height for Alex who buried her face between Maggie's legs. Maggie gripped her shoulders while her tongue worked its magic. Maggie cried out quietly as she rode the waves of orgasms.

"And now," Alex said. "It's time for me to take you home again. Will I see you before Sunday?"

"No. I think we should wait until Sunday."

"Okay. If that's what you think is best."

"I do."

They drove back to the convent in silence.

"Today was wonderful," Alex finally said. "I love our stolen moments."

"So do I. Thank you for everything."

"My pleasure."

Maggie got out of the truck and went in to have dinner with her sisters.

The following morning, after breakfast, Maggie went to the church. It was dark and cool and quiet. It fit her mood. Since God wasn't answering her when she prayed in her room, she decided it was time to talk to Him in His house. She crossed herself as she walked in and genuflected reverently before taking a seat in the front pew.

She dropped to her knees and rested her forehead on her clasped hands. She prayed with all her might. She said prayer after prayer and interspersed them with pleas for Him to give her guidance and show her what to do regarding Alex.

Her stomach growled, and she checked her watch. It was five o'clock. She'd been at it all day and had no more answers than she had when she'd started. She got up, crossed herself, and left the church.

She questioned, as had become the norm, what she was doing with Alex. It felt so right, how could it be wrong? And if God wasn't giving her any new direction in which to go, did that mean He was okay with Alex and her? It made her brain hurt to think so much.

Maggie prayed some more in her room to pass the time until dinner. When six o'clock rolled around, she got up and went to the dining room.

"Hello, Maggie," Reverend Mother said to her. "I haven't seen you all day. Where have you been?"

"I was in the church, praying."

"And did it help?"

"Not really."

"Well," Reverend Mother said, "I don't know how His powers work, obviously, but if you need a mere mortal to talk to, I'm always available."

"Thank you, Reverend Mother."

The nuns sat down, and Reverend Mother said grace. Maggie dug into her dinner. She was famished. It wasn't like her to miss lunch, but she'd been busy. She listened to the chatter around her and wanted to join in, but felt distanced from her sisters. They were all devout, faithful women. Why couldn't she be?

And then she wondered if they were all as devout as she thought. After all, she was devout, but not so faithful anymore and none of them would have guessed that about her. No one but Reverend Mother, that was. How much did she know? And should Maggie just talk to her?

No, she decided. This problem was between God and her. Nobody else needed to be involved.

Saturday morning, Maggie went to breakfast late. She'd overslept, which was unusual for her. This meant she had the dining room to herself, as the food was being put away when she got there. She had a yogurt and a muffin and ate them quickly.

After breakfast, Maggie went to the garden to cut flowers to put in the large flower holders located on the steps leading to the altar. She arranged them just so and then took her place in the front pew again to pray.

She continued to pray until the musicians for the five thirty Mass showed up to rehearse. She crossed herself and went back to her room. Instead of praying, she lay on her bed and thought of Alex. She loved her. There was no doubt. She was head over heels in love with her. But she also loved God. Why did things have to be so complicated?

She joined the other nuns for dinner and then went to her room and went to bed. Granted, it was early, but she was mentally and emotionally exhausted and fell into a deep sleep.

Chapter Fifteen

Maggie woke up Sunday morning excited about the day. It was her day with Alex, and nothing would get her down. She wasn't alone in the showers, but they each had their own stalls, so she didn't mind. She dressed quickly and went to breakfast. The morning seemed to drag on interminably until finally, it was time to go to Mass.

She stood in her usual spot with the other nuns and sang the processional hymn, but she never took her gaze away from the side entrance. She finally saw Alex walk in and smiled widely. Alex smiled back at her and Maggie felt her heart skip a beat.

The hymn finally ended, and Maggie turned her attention to the priest. She focused almost completely on the Mass, though the knowledge that Alex was there was never far from her mind.

When Mass ended, Maggie crossed the church to see Alex.

"How are you?" Maggie said.

"I'm good. And you?"

"Much better now."

Alex grinned at her.

"Shouldn't you be at the social?"

"I should. Walk with me?"

"Sure."

They each took a doughnut.

"Shouldn't you be socializing?" Alex said.

"I suppose I should."

"Go for it. I'm not going anywhere."

"Thanks, I will."

Maggie made the rounds through the crowd, stopping to visit with the usual parishioners as well as meeting new people who were just visiting. She glanced over at Alex and saw Reverend Mother talking to her. Maggie's heart was in her throat. What could Reverend Mother possibly have to say to Alex? She certainly hoped she wasn't discussing their relationship. She was a nervous wreck and made her way back through the crowd to where the women stood.

"Hello," Maggie said.

"Hello," Reverend Mother said. "We were just discussing the trip you two took together."

"Ah, yes," Maggie said. "I showed Reverend Mother our pictures."

"I hope you were as impressed as we were," Alex said.

"Oh, I was. And jealous? I know that's not a pretty trait, but I am so jealous. That's the trip of a lifetime."

"That it was," Alex said.

"I think it's wonderful that you took Maggie with you."

"I didn't want to go alone."

"And you had no friends or family you could have taken?"

Maggie's stomach was in knots. She felt like Reverend Mother was grilling Alex, trying to make her slip up.

"No one I would have rather taken. I mean, sure I could have asked a friend, but no one I know would have gotten as much out of it as Sister Mary Margaret. She appreciated the sanctity of all the places we visited."

"That I did," Maggie said.

"Well, thank you again for taking her," Reverend Mother said. "I should mingle some more, though the place is clearing out rather quickly."

"Shall we start cleaning up?" Maggie said.

"Yes, please."

Maggie and Alex busied themselves cleaning up, then went to Maggie's room for Maggie to change. They got in Alex's truck.

"So, what happened back there?" Alex said.

"What do you mean?"

"You looked terrified when you saw me talking to your mother superior. Do you not trust me to keep our secret?"

"Of course I trust you," Maggie said. "It's her I worry about."

"How so?"

"She's been asking me questions about you and me and my vows."

"Oh, shit."

"Yeah."

"I'm sorry, Mags. Why didn't you tell me?"

"I wanted to handle it on my own," Maggie said.

Alex was silent for a moment.

"Look, no matter how complicated things are, I like to think of us as a couple," she said. "That means working through our troubles together."

"I understand. I'm sorry."

"So what exactly has she said?"

"Well," Maggie said. "She's hinted at us seeing each other and reminded me that my vow of chastity applied to women as well as men."

"Damn. She really is on to us, isn't she?"

"I'm afraid so."

They pulled up in front of Alex's house.

"Let's finish this conversation inside," Alex said.

They went in, and Alex poured them each a glass of wine.

"I know it's early," she said. "But I figure it can't hurt."

"No. I need the fortification."

"Me, too. So, what are we going to do, Mags? I mean, well, what I mean is what are we going to do?"

"I don't know, Alex. I've prayed so hard for guidance, but none is forthcoming. I love you, but I love the Church, too. I don't know what to do."

"Should we stop seeing each other?" Alex said.

"I think that would break my heart."

"Good answer. It would crush mine."

"So where does that leave us?"

"I guess we just keep doing what we're doing," Alex said. "Because I love you and need you."

"I need you, too. Now, enough talking. Let's go to your room."

They took the stairs slowly, and when they got to Alex's room, they undressed each other leisurely and deliberately. When they were naked together, Alex pulled Maggie close. She kissed her softly, tenderly.

"I love you so much," she said.

"I love you, too."

Alex kissed her again, and Maggie opened her mouth inviting Alex inside. Their tongues frolicked together, and Maggie felt her heat rise. She needed Alex with every ounce of her being. She was wet and ready. She pulled away, lay on the bed, and beckoned Alex to join her.

Alex climbed on top of her and kissed her passionately. Maggie returned the kiss fiercely, conveying the very depths of her need in that kiss.

"Wow," Alex said when they came up for air. "That was some kiss."

"Yeah, it was."

Alex kissed her again, briefly, before she moved down Maggie's body to take a nipple in her mouth. She felt it grow as she sucked on it. She pressed it against the roof of her mouth and played over it with her tongue.

She finally released it and continued to kiss down Maggie's body. She tongued her belly button and made Maggie squirm. She kissed lower yet and positioned herself between Maggie's legs.

"I love making love to you," she said.

"I love it when you do."

"Good."

Alex lowered her head and buried her face between Maggie's legs. She dragged her tongue along the length of her before sucking and licking her lips. They were swollen and juicy, and she played with them a long time.

"Oh, my God, you feel good," Maggie said.

Alex dipped her tongue as deep inside Maggie as it would go. She lapped at her walls before she moved to her clit. It, too, was swollen and Alex took it between her lips to suck it while she slipped her fingers inside her.

Maggie bucked against Alex, urging her deeper. She lost all conscious thought. She could only feel, and feel she did. She felt Alex's actions to her core. And in her core, a mass of heat was forming. She concentrated on the heat and Alex, and finally the mass broke loose, shooting heat over her limbs as she climaxed forcefully.

"Oh, my God, you love me so well," Maggie said. Alex withdrew her hand and moved so she was lying next to Maggie.

"I love loving you," she said.

"Lucky me."

Maggie kissed her and tasted herself on Alex's lips. She slid her hand down Alex's body and pried her legs open. Alex was happy to oblige. She spread wider and lay back to let Maggie do her thing.

Maggie slipped her fingers deep inside Alex. She twisted and turned her hand as she pulled it out then pushed it back in. Alex moved with her and soon was calling out Maggie's name as she came.

They lay together quietly for a while. Maggie loved listening to Alex breathing. It was so soothing to her. She curled up in her arms and pressed her ear against her chest. She listened to her strong heartbeat and knew she was home.

After a few minutes, Alex stirred.

"You ready for a swim?" she said.

"Sure. Let's do it."

They hit the water. It felt good on Maggie's still warm skin. The sun and the pool always revitalized her. She swam for a while with Alex, then settled in to watch her finish her laps. Alex swam over to where Maggie sat.

"The water feels good today, doesn't it?" she said.

"It always does. I love your pool."

"Good. You look good in it."

"Thanks. So do you."

They got out of the pool and lay on lounge chairs.

"This is nice," Maggie said.

"It is. Though I have to admit, I don't know how long I can lie here next to you and not take you. You're just too gorgeous for words."

Maggie blushed.

"Aw. Thank you. So are you, you know. Gorgeous, I mean."

"Thanks. I'm glad you think so."

They relaxed in the sun for a while in silence. Alex broke it.

"So, do I get to see you Tuesday and Thursday again this week?" she said.

"Sure. Although summer school starts the week after, so we'll be back to just Sundays."

Alex was quiet for a beat.

"Well," she said. "That bites."

"I know. I'm sorry."

"No. Don't apologize. You're a nun first. I get that. I don't always like it, but I get it."

"Thank you for understanding. Have you ever thought what it would be like if I left the convent?"

Alex propped herself up on an elbow to look at Maggie.

"I could never ask you to do that," she said.

"I know. It's just, well, sometimes I wonder what it would be like to spend every day and every night with you. Does that scare you?"

"I feel like it should, but it doesn't. I think I'd like that very much. Unfortunately, it's not going to happen. And I know that."

"I wish I could be as sure as you are," Maggie said.

"What's that supposed to mean?"

"It just means I wish God would show me a sign to let me know what I'm supposed to do. Like, does He want me to stay in the convent? Or does He want me to leave and pursue my happiness with you?"

"I think you're the only one that can answer that, Mags."

"But don't you see? I can't do it on my own. I need His guidance."

"Do you?"

"I do," Maggie said. "I've always prayed for guidance, and He's never let me down before. I just wish He'd send me a sign now."

"Not to change the subject," Alex said. "Baloney. This is indeed to change the subject. I think we're dry enough for dinner, don't you?"

"Sure," Maggie said. She wanted to talk some more with Alex, but clearly she was making her uncomfortable. Maybe Alex didn't love her as much as she loved Alex. No, she didn't buy that. She knew Alex loved her equally as much as she loved Alex.

"I'll go get the steaks if you want to grab the salad and plates and things. Oh, and will you pour us each another glass of wine?"

"You got it."

Maggie did as she was asked and was soon sitting at the patio table watching Alex working the grill. She admired her muscular back and toned butt. Her fingers itched to touch her. She got up and ran her hand down Alex's back. She leaned into it, pressing her breasts against her.

"Hey there," Alex said. "I do like the feel of that."

"It's so hard to keep my hands off of you."

"Well, hold that thought. Dinner is ready."

They ate and talked and laughed and relaxed after their in-depth conversation earlier. They sipped their wine and Maggie felt herself grow mellow. And horny. She couldn't wait until dinner was over so she could have her way with Alex.

When the dishes were washed and dried, Maggie took Alex's hand.

"Come on," she said. She led her upstairs to Alex's bedroom. She pushed Alex playfully, and Alex lay on the bed. She pulled Maggie on top of her. They kissed like mad women. It was a kiss filled with desire and need. Maggie needed more. She ground into Alex, but she could feel the ball coalescing in her center again and needed something to help get her off.

Alex bent her knee and Maggie ground into it for all she was worth. She moved up and down, all the while pressing her swollen clit into Alex's leg. She continued what she was doing until the ball inside burst open and sent white-hot chills all over her body. She collapsed on top of Alex.

"Wow," she said. "That was something else."

"Yeah, it was. You're so fucking hot."

"Thank you. I feel rather wanton after that little display."

"Nonsense. No way. It was hotter than hell."

"Well, thank you. I needed that."

"Now," Alex said. "You just relax and let me take you there again."

Maggie rolled off Alex, who quickly took her place between her legs. She licked and sucked and licked and sucked some more. No inch of Maggie was left unattended. She moved her mouth to Maggie's clit and sucked on it hard as she slid her fingers as deep as they would go. In and out, she moved them while she sucked on Maggie. Maggie pressed her face into her as she cried out and rode the orgasms that cascaded over her body.

"Oh, man," Maggie said. "You sure know what you're doing."

"I'm just having fun. You do the rest."

"I just lie there."

"Nonsense. The way you move tells me just what you need when you need it. I simply pay attention."

"Well, I'm glad you do."

Maggie took a moment to catch her breath, then climbed between Alex's legs. She sucked Alex's lips and ran her tongue between them. Alex moved against her, letting her know she was on the right track. Maggie strained her tongue trying to lick all the soft spots inside Alex. She finally sucked her clit while she slipped her fingers inside her. In no time, Alex called Maggie's name as she climaxed over and over again.

They lay quietly again until Alex spoke.

"Mags? Hey, Mags, are you awake?"

"I'm awake. And I see the clock."

"Yeah, bummer, but I need to get you home."

They dressed and walked out to the truck.

"So, Tuesday for sure, right?" Alex said.

"Yep. At least for a couple of hours."

"If that's all I get, I'll take it."

"Well, that's all I can give. Sorry."

"Mags, don't worry. It's the nature of our relationship. And I knew it going into this with you. So don't say you're sorry. Don't be sorry. It's all good, okay?"

"If you say so."

"I say so."

Alex dropped Maggie off at the convent.

"I'll see you Tuesday," she said.

"See you then."

Maggie went into her room and undressed. She plopped on her bed and was soon sound asleep with dreams of Alex dancing in her head.

Chapter Sixteen

Tuesday after lunch, Maggie went to work weeding the garden again. She lost track of time, and suddenly a shadow fell over her. She looked up to see Alex standing there.

"Oh, my. I had no idea it was this late. I'm sorry I'm not dressed better."

"It's okay. Come on, though. I don't want to miss any of our time together. You can shower at my place."

Maggie looked around to make sure there were no curious ears in the area. She saw no one, so she nodded at Alex.

"That's a good idea. Let's go."

She climbed into Alex's truck.

"Sorry about getting your truck dirty," Maggie said.

"Oh, hon. Look around you. My truck is filthy. Always has been since I bought it. Don't you worry about a few specks of dirt."

"Okay. If you insist.

"I do. Besides, this way, we both need showers, so it's a good thing you're sitting in my truck covered in dirt," Alex said.

"Yes. This is true. And a shower with you sounds like the perfect way to get things started."

"Yes, it does."

They arrived at Alex's house and, once inside, Alex kissed Maggie on the lips.

"No time for this," Maggie said. "We need to get clean."

"So be it," Alex said. "Come on."

They went upstairs, and Alex turned on the water while she watched Maggie strip. Maggie stood naked before her, and she felt all her sensitive spots harden under Alex's scrutiny. She was dripping wet and hoped Alex couldn't see the evidence of her arousal running down her leg.

"You're gorgeous," Alex said and closed the distance between them.

"Oh, no you don't. You need to lose your clothes, too."

"Fair enough." She climbed out of her clothes and pulled Maggie to her. "Now. Now, I get you."

She kissed her hard on her mouth before guiding her into the shower. She lathered Maggie up and slipped her fingers inside her. She stroked her deep and furiously until Maggie collapsed against the shower wall, spent.

Maggie dropped to her knees and worked her tongue in and out of Alex until Alex cried out as she came.

They rinsed, dried, and took their lovemaking to the bedroom where Alex climbed between Maggie's legs. She lapped at her, delving her tongue deep inside her before moving it to her clit. Maggie screamed Alex's name as she climaxed again and again.

"God, I've missed you," Alex said as she moved up to take Maggie in her arms. "I don't know what I'm going to do when we're back to Sundays only."

"I know. It's going to be hard. But we can do it. We did it before and we can do it again."

"Yeah. I know we can. It'll be hard. But I agree. We can do it."

Maggie ran her hand over Alex's taut body and brought it to rest between her legs.

"Mm," she said. "I love how wet you always are for me."

"That's because you excite me so much. I can't get over how turned on I get with you."

"That makes me feel good," Maggie said. She slid her fingers inside Alex and ran her fingers around inside of her. "You're so tight. I love being inside you."

"I love it when you're in me, so we're even."

"Mm." Maggie slipped her hand out, then twisted it and re-entered her. She repeated this several times until Alex reached her orgasms.

They lay together in each other's arms.

"Have you prayed any more about us?" Alex said.

"I pray every day. Why?"

"Just wondered if you had any answers."

"None yet."

"I don't want you to get in trouble," Alex said.

"Why would I get in trouble?"

"You know, your mother superior was asking questions. I just don't want her figuring us out and coming down on you."

"I don't think she'll come down on me, per se."

"She might make you choose," Alex said. "And I don't want you to have to do that."

"I don't want to have to do that, either. I love you, Alex, and can't imagine my life without you."

"I feel the same way."

"But I can't imagine my life not serving the Lord."

"I get that, too."

"It's such a hard call," Maggie said. "How can loving you be wrong?"

"I don't know. I suppose if I was a bigger person, I'd walk away and leave you in peace."

Maggie panicked.

"You wouldn't do that would you?"

"No. I'm not that big of a person. And I love you too much to just walk away from what we have."

"I'm glad to hear that."

"Do you want to go to the pool?" Alex said.

"No. I just want to lie here with you today."

"Sounds good to me. I could make love to you all day."

Alex dragged her hand down Maggie's body to where her legs met. She slid between them and rubbed Maggie's clit. She was slick but not as swollen as usual. That quickly changed at Alex's ministrations. Soon Maggie was crying out Alex's name as she climaxed.

Maggie lay contentedly in Alex's arms. She knew she should return the favor, but she wasn't ready. Not yet. She still had too much on her brain.

"Are you lost in your head?" Alex said.

"Yeah. I'm sorry."

"It's okay. I'm okay. I don't need attention right now. I don't need it until you're ready."

"I'm still sorry. I find your body irresistible. I shouldn't worry so much. I should just enjoy you."

"Sh. It's okay. You just lie here with me and I'll be okay."

"You're too good to me," Maggie said.

"Nah. I just love you. That's all."

"Well, I appreciate that. And I appreciate you. And I think I'm ready to show you how much."

"Only if you're ready."

"I am."

Maggie climbed between Alex's legs. Suddenly nothing else mattered. She and Alex were all alone, and Alex lay there waiting for Maggie to please her. Maggie placed Alex's legs over her shoulders as she bent to taste her. She loved how good Alex tasted. She couldn't get enough of her. She licked deep inside her, lapping at her juices. She moved her mouth to her clit and slid her fingers inside her.

Alex bucked against Maggie as she loved her. Maggie moved her fingers in and out as she sucked on Alex's clit. Alex pressed Maggie's face to her. Maggie fought for air but didn't stop. She kept going until she heard her name screamed from deep inside Alex.

She moved up next to Alex and curled into her waiting arms.

"Hey, Mags?" Alex said.

"Yeah?"

"We need to get you back to the convent."

"Is it time?"

"Yeah. I'm sorry."

"It's okay," Maggie said. "I'm glad someone was paying attention to the time. Let's get dressed."

Maggie put on her dirty clothes and watched as Alex donned clean shorts and a clean shirt. Alex dropped Maggie off just in time for her to change into something clean and go to dinner.

Reverend Mother said grace, and they all ate. Everyone was enjoying their light duties before summer school began. The conversations were easy, and Maggie relaxed and enjoyed the synergy of being with her sisters.

The following day, Maggie was in her room working on her lesson plans for the following week when there was a knock on her door. She opened it to find Reverend Mother standing in the hall.

"Please, come in, Reverend Mother."

"Thank you. How are you today, Maggie?"

"I'm great. I'm working on lesson plans for summer school. I'm excited to get back in the classroom again."

"Good. I'm glad to hear that. Maggie, I have to ask you a question."

"Yes, ma'am?" Maggie's stomach was in knots, but she did her best to play it cool.

"Are you happy, Maggie?"

"Yes, ma'am."

"I mean, really, really happy?"

"Reverend Mother, I've never been in a better space in my life." Granted, she was confused, but she loved serving her Lord and loved loving Alex. For the moment, she had the best of both worlds, and she was very happy.

"I'm glad to hear that. Because I'm really worried about you."

"How so?" She didn't think she wanted to hear the answer.

"I worry about your relationship with Alex Foster."

"What's to worry about?"

"Maggie," Mother Superior said. "Temptation comes in all forms, all shapes and sizes. A handsome woman is just one form it can take."

"Alex is just a good friend," Maggie lied. "That's all there is to it."

"I want to believe you. But you spend an inordinate amount of time with her. I can't help but wonder."

"You don't need to wonder. Alex's a good Catholic, and I'm a good nun."

"I hope so. I just don't want you breaking your vows. It's easy to do. You see, Maggie, I, too, was once tempted."

"You were?"

"Yes," Reverend Mother said. "And I thought I was safe because she was a woman. How could I be attracted to a woman?"

Maggie had no idea what to say. Reverend Mother went on.

"But I was. At first, we were friends. I loved hanging out with her. I came close to shirking my duties to be with her. I didn't, but I was tempted. Every chance we got, we hung out together. It wasn't until one evening when she kissed me that I realized I was in trouble."

"Reverend Mother, you don't need to tell me this."

"Ah, but I do. At least, I feel like I do. I don't want you to be tricked. Alex Foster seems like a very nice woman. But she's very masculine, and I question her sexuality. Obviously, I have nothing against lesbians, but I don't think you should be spending as much time with her as you have been."

"Well, once school starts, I won't be. So you should be happy."

"Can I ask you to give up your Sundays with her?"

Maggie drew in a deep breath.

"I don't know that I want to do that. It's nice to get a break, you know? To get away from the convent for a few hours. And it's been warm lately, and her pool feels wonderful."

"Maggie. Please. Be careful. I don't want to lose you. You're a good nun."

"I'll be careful. I'm a big girl, Reverend Mother. I can take care of myself."

"Maggie, I've seen the way you two look at each other. I can't do anything more for you. I've given you my advice. I'll tell you my door's always open if you want to talk. But I don't want you to think you're pulling the wool over my eyes."

Maggie's heart leaped to her throat. She'd seen the way they looked at each other? She'd always thought they were so careful. Maybe Reverend Mother was just fishing. Stay cool, she told herself.

"I don't know what you think you see, but I assure you there's nothing between us besides a good friendship," Maggie said.

"Don't fool yourself, Maggie. And don't let her fool you. I suggest you pray long and hard over your relationship with her."

"There's no relationship to pray over."

"Okay. Maybe I should have said your friendship."

"I will, Reverend Mother."

"Thank you," Reverend Mother said. "And, again, if you need to talk, please don't hesitate to contact me."

"Thank you."

Reverend Mother left, and Maggie placed her head in her hands and took some deep breaths. She was determined not to cry. Reverend Mother knew. What did this mean for her and Alex?

Thursday, Maggie met Alex at her truck in the parking lot.

"How are you today?" Alex said.

"Pretty good."

"Just pretty good? Not great? I'm great because I'm with you now."

"Oh, Alex. It's wonderful to be with you. You know that."

"I like to hear it," Alex said.

"Okay. It's great to see you, Alex."

"Thanks." Alex smiled at her. "How have things been for you since I last saw you?"

"Reverend Mother came by to see me yesterday."

"Oh, yeah?"

"Yeah."

"What did she want?" Alex said.

"She wanted to talk about us."

"Oh. Is that right? And what did she have to say about us?"

"She said she's seen the way we look at each other," Maggie said.

"That's bullshit. I'm always careful not to let my love for you show when we're in public. I make sure my eyes aren't all lovey-dovey."

They arrived at Alex's house. Alex let them in and took Maggie's hand.

"Let's have wine," she said. She poured them each a glass, and they sat on the couch in the living room. "So, you want to talk about it?"

"I don't know what to say. She said she was once tempted by a woman, so she knows what I'm going through."

"Your mother superior is a lesbian?"

"She said they started as friends and one time the woman kissed her."

"Wow. That's hard for me to wrap my brain around."

"Yeah. So, she gets it. She knows what I'm going through, or so she said," Maggie said.

"So did you come clean about us?"

"Heck, no. I told her we're just friends. She wants me to give up my Sundays with you, and I told her I wouldn't."

"I'm so sorry, Mags. I hate complicating your life like this."

"Sure, you complicate it, but you also enrich it, and I wouldn't trade you for anything."

"I hope you mean that," Alex said.

"I do."

They sipped their wine in silence for a few minutes.

"So, how have you been?" Maggie said.

"I've been good. Working hard, missing you. The usual."

"Sounds about right."

"You want some more wine?" Alex said.

"No. I think I'd rather have you."

Maggie stood and slowly undressed. When she was naked, she offered her hand to Alex, who took it and stood. Alex stripped and pulled Maggie to her.

"I love the feel of your skin against mine," Alex said.

"So do I. Except I'm always afraid I'll overheat."

Alex eased Maggie down on the couch and climbed on top of her. She pressed her knee to her center as she kissed her passionately. Maggie ground into Alex's knee but needed more. She took one of Alex's hands and placed it between her legs.

Alex moved her fingers in and out until Maggie cried out as the orgasms cascaded over her. She rolled over until she was on top of Alex. She kissed down her body until she was between her legs. Alex placed one leg over the back of the couch and one over Maggie's shoulder.

Maggie dipped her face and licked Alex all over. She buried her tongue as deep inside Alex as it would go before she sucked her clit until Alex called her name.

Chapter Seventeen

Sunday rolled around, and Maggie met up with Alex during the social.

"How was the rest of your week?" Alex said.

"It was good. I worked in the garden a lot. And worked on lesson plans. I think I'm ready for summer school to start tomorrow. How was yours?"

Alex opened her mouth to answer, but Maggie cut her off by walking away. She'd seen Reverend Mother approaching them, and she wasn't in the mood to deal with her accusations, true though they may be. She cut through the crowd and mingled, concentrating as best she could, but her gaze kept going back to Alex who Reverend Mother had trapped.

Maggie saw Reverend Mother walk off and made her way back through the crowd to Alex.

"Sorry about that. I couldn't face her," Maggie said.

Alex laughed.

"It's all good. As soon as I saw her I knew why you'd bailed."

"What did she have to say to you?"

"Nothing, really. We just talked about the Mass today and the message in it. No biggie."

"Good. I'm glad."

"She also told me what an outstanding nun you are," Alex said. "I told her I got that from you. She also said how valuable you are to the convent and the school."

"Wow. She was going for the major guilt trip, huh?"

"Yep. But I was cool under pressure. No worries about that."

"Thank you."

"No problem," Alex said. "Now, shall we start cleaning up so we can get out of here?"

They finished putting everything away and cut through the garden to Maggie's room, where she quickly changed her clothes. Maggie was careful, as always, to bring her bathing suit and towel to avoid suspicion. She opened her door and found Reverend Mother standing there.

"Hello," Reverend Mother said.

"Hello. We were just on our way out," Maggie said. "Was there something I could help you with?"

"I was hoping I could have dinner with you tonight," Reverend Mother said.

"We kind of had plans."

"I do hope you're flexible. I'd very much like to take you to dinner."

"It's fine by me," Alex said. "We can just swim for a while and I can have you back here whenever."

"Great. We'll leave at six," Mother Superior said. "Meet me at my office."

"I'll be there," Maggie said. She watched Reverend Mother walk down the hall and fought to keep from murmuring an expletive.

They got out to the truck. When their doors were closed, Maggie was close to tears.

"Why can't she just leave me alone?" she said. "She has no proof that I'm anything but an exemplary nun."

"She just wants to be sure, Mags. Don't worry. She's not going to hurt you. There's no way. She probably just wants to ask you some more questions."

"I doubt it. She's just trying to keep me away from you. And I don't appreciate it."

"That could be. But do you blame her? She thinks she's going to lose you to me and she doesn't want that happening. She's going to do everything in her power to keep you. I don't blame her."

"I guess I don't, either. But I hate being alone with her. I hate lying to her. I hate denying my love for you. I feel like I'm being unfaithful to you."

"Oh, Mags." Alex took her hand as they pulled into her driveway. "You're not being unfaithful to me. You're doing what you need to ensure we can stay together. I realize it's not easy, and I wish to God I could take the stress off you, but I can't. Only you can deal with it. And I'm sure you'll be fine."

They went inside.

"You want wine? I realize it's early."

"I'd love a glass of wine. Thanks."

They sat on the couch and sipped their wine.

"God, I don't want our time cut short today. Sundays are my favorite days of the week," Maggie said. "I don't want to miss dinner with you to have dinner with her."

"I know, Mags. I know."

"It's just not fair."

"I hear you. Do you need to cry?"

"No. Thanks. I thought for sure I would earlier, but I'm okay now."

"Good," Alex said. "You want to go upstairs?"

"Yes. Please. I need to be with you."

They walked upstairs, and Alex carefully undressed Maggie. She then disrobed and eased Maggie onto the bed.

"I bought us something," Alex said. She walked to the dresser and walked back to the bed.

"What did you buy us?"

Alex held up a pink toy.

"Oh, my," Maggie blushed. "How does that work?"

Alex motioned first to the large bulbous part.

"This goes inside you." She pointed to the thinner, shorter section. "And this goes against your clit. I can adjust the speed and pulsing. I think you're going to love it."

"I'm a little nervous. I'll be honest," Maggie said.

"Well, let me make love to you first. We'll get you nice and wet before we use the toy, okay?"

Maggie nodded.

Alex lay on top of Maggie and kissed her, hard at first, but then softly and tenderly.

"I love you," she said.

"I love you."

Alex continued to kiss Maggie as she skimmed her hand over her body. She brought her hand to rest on one of her breasts. She pinched her nipple and twisted it before she moved her hand lower. Maggie was wet, and Alex entered her easily. She moved in and out, and Maggie lost the sense of anything but Alex and the feelings she was creating. She closed her eyes tight and saw flecks of light flickering behind her eyelids. Finally, the colors burst out and flooded her eyelids as Maggie reached a gut-wrenching climax. She lay with her eyes closed as her world came back together. She heard a buzzing sound.

"Mags?" Alex said.

"Hm?"

"I'm going to put the toy inside you now, okay?"

"Okay."

Alex eased the tip inside her.

"Oh, my," Maggie said. "That feels good."

"Yeah? Okay. I'm going to push it in deeper now."

"Okay."

"Oh, yeah. That's nice," Maggie said.

Alex turned on the clit stimulator.

"Ooh. Oh, yes. Oh, God, that feels good."

"Excellent. Now just relax and let the toy do all the work." She eased the toy in and out while she held the stimulator against Maggie's clit.

Maggie moved up and down against the toy, while she reached down and helped hold the stimulator in place.

"Oh, my God, that feels so good," Maggie said. "Oh, my God, I'm so close."

"Yeah? Come for me, baby," Alex said. "Let it out. Show me that you love me."

"Oh, God, yes!" Maggie cried out as she came again and again. When she could breathe normally, Alex still couldn't take the toy out of her.

"You've still got quite a grip on it," she said. "I don't think I can ease it out yet."

"I'm sorry. But will you please turn off the stimulator? I've had my fill and it hurts."

"Oh, sorry about that."

Alex pressed the button and held it down to turn the toy off. She could finally ease it out of Maggie, and she set it on the bed next to them. She took Maggie in her arms.

"So, you like the toy?" she said.

"Oh, yeah. That was fun."

"Good."

"And now I get to use it on you, right?"

"Sure. Go for it."

Maggie positioned herself between Alex's legs and eased the toy inside her.

"This doesn't hurt, does it?"

"No. It feels amazing. Don't be shy, Mags."

"Okay."

Maggie turned the clit stimulator on and pressed it into Alex. She moved the toy in and out of her, while she kept the stimulator firmly in place. It wasn't easy, but she did it, and soon Alex was calling her name as she reached her orgasms.

"That was awesome," Alex said. "Just incredible."

"Right on. I'm glad it worked for you."

"Take it out and come up here to snuggle with me."

Maggie did as instructed and curled into Alex's arms. She lay in comfort there until she felt her eyelids growing heavy.

"I'm about to fall asleep here," she said.

"Oh, that won't do. I need to get you back to the convent."

"Yeah. I guess you do, but not right now. Let's swim for a while."

"That sounds good."

They went to the pool and swam a few laps. Maggie had woken up and was feeling better.

"How you doin'?" Alex said when she swam over next to Maggie.

"I'm okay. Nervous, but okay."

"I wish I could make the nerves go away."

"You already helped tremendously. I'm not as uptight as I was. Making love with you always relaxes me."

"Good. That's my job. And I love it."

"You're very good at your job," Maggie said.

Alex kissed her then. It was a tender kiss that conveyed so much in the few seconds it lasted.

"I love you," Maggie said.

"I love you, too."

"I love kissing you."

"Good. Because there's plenty more where that came from."

They dried off in the sun, and soon it was time for Alex to drive Maggie home.

"We'd better get dressed," Alex said.

"Yeah. I suppose we should."

"I hate to do that. I love lying around nude with you."

"I enjoy it, too. Very much. But it wouldn't do to keep Reverend Mother waiting."

"And I won't see you again until Sunday," Alex said.

"That's right. Summer school starts tomorrow."

"It's going to be a long week."

"We'll make it."

"Yeah. We don't have a choice."

They dressed quietly and drove back to the convent. Alex gave Maggie's hand a squeeze when they got there.

"Good luck with dinner," she said.

"Thanks."

"Will you at least call me sometime during the week? I'd like to hear how dinner goes."

"I'll try, but I can't promise anything. Especially with Reverend Mother watching me like a hawk."

"Oh, yeah. That's true. Okay. Well, then, I'll just plan on seeing you Sunday."

"Yeah. Sunday," Maggie said.

"I know it's a long way away, but we'll make it. And I promise to make it worth your while."

"I do like the sound of that. Okay. I need to go inside now."

"Okay. I love you, Mags."

"I love you, too."

Maggie went inside and changed her clothes for dinner. The knot in her stomach was back in full force. She doubted she'd even be able to eat due to her nerves. But she had no choice but to go, so she walked down the hall to Reverend Mother's office.

"Ah, Maggie. You're ready," Reverend Mother said.

"Yes, ma'am. Where are we going?"

"Palazzo Giuseppe. I've been craving Italian ever since you went to Italy. I'm sure the food won't be as good as what you got there, but it's supposed to be tasty."

They got in Reverend Mother's car and drove to the restaurant. The décor was nice, with the large plate glass windows overlooking the street. When they were seated, Reverend Mother simply looked at Maggie, who was growing more nervous with each passing moment. She finally found her voice.

"So, to what do I owe this dinner, Reverend Mother?" she said.

"I think we need to talk. And I wanted to do it away from the convent."

"Is this about Alex Foster again, because—"

Reverend Mother held up her hand.

"Maggie, after Mass today, you moved away from her when you saw me approaching. I wonder if that was a sign of guilt."

"No guilt. I just needed to mingle. She's a very dear friend. Probably my only friend. Definitely my only friend outside of the convent. And it would be easy to talk to her and ignore my duties to the rest of the parishioners. So, I left her to mingle."

"But you did it as soon as you saw me walking up. I couldn't help but notice the timing."

"I'm sorry. I didn't notice."

"Maggie, our eyes met. You knew I was coming your way. I won't tolerate your lying to me. And I think you're lying to me and maybe even to yourself where Ms. Foster is concerned."

"I'm not. I know what you think. You think I'm weak and would easily give in to the sins of the flesh, but I'm not. Our relationship isn't like that." Maggie was surprised at how easily she could lie to Reverend Mother. But she didn't care. She was mad. Mad at her for figuring it out and mad at her for calling her on it. She wouldn't give in, though. She wouldn't admit defeat.

"I don't think you're weak, Maggie. I don't think that at all. But as I've said before, sometimes temptations arise without our noticing, and before we know it, we're giving in to them. It's happened to me, and I happen to think I'm very devout."

"I know you are."

"And I think you are, too. I just don't want to see you get sideswiped."

"I won't."

"I'd like you to talk to Father Bremer," Reverend Mother said.

"What would I say? That you're worried about my relationship with a parishioner that's strictly platonic?"

"Maggie, I've seen the way she looks at you. And I swear I've seen you look at her the same way. But if I'm wrong about you, I'm not wrong about the way she watches you. She's crazy about you. And I don't know her well enough to know if she's strong enough not to act on her feelings."

"Then you'll just have to trust me not to let her."

Their dinners arrived, and Maggie took a bite. It tasted like cardboard. She was sure it was delicious, but her appetite was gone.

"This is really good," Reverend Mother said. "Does it compare to what you ate in Italy?"

"Yeah. It really does." Maggie felt horrible that the lies just kept coming.

"Oh, good. I was afraid you'd be disappointed. Don't you usually have dinner with Alex on Sundays? What do you usually eat?"

"She usually grills something. Steak or fish usually. And we have a salad and some wine with it. It's nice."

"And she has a pool? So you get to swim every week?"

"Yes, ma'am. I love to swim. And the weather's been so unseasonably warm that the pool's felt really good."

"What else do you do when you're over there?"

Maggie blushed. Damn it. She looked down to hide her face, but Mother Superior had seen.

"What was the blush for? If it's all innocent and on the up-and-up, why the need to blush?"

"I just felt like you were implying something," Maggie said.

"Well, I wasn't. But I am now more convinced than ever that there's more to your relationship than you're admitting."

"There's not. I promise."

"I hope not, Maggie. As I've said before, I'd hate to lose you."

"You're not going to lose me."

"I think it's about time for you to make a choice. You need to choose her or the Church."

"I don't think I need to make a choice," Maggie said.

"I think you do. I'll let it go for now so we can enjoy our dinner, but this isn't our last discussion on this matter, Maggie."

Maggie didn't eat another bite. She fought tears as she moved her food around on her plate. She couldn't choose between Alex and the Church. She just couldn't.

CHAPTER EIGHTEEN

Maggie threw herself into teaching the next week. She got up every morning, ate breakfast, grabbed a sack lunch, and went to school. She taught her classes, ate her lunch, and stayed after school to grade class work. Anything to keep her away from Reverend Mother. She couldn't face her. How dare she tell Maggie to make that choice. She couldn't stand to be around her. She was so angry.

But dinner rolled around every evening and she had to be in the dining room with her. She went out of her way not to sit by her, and Reverend Mother never sought her out. For that, she was deeply relieved.

Friday afternoon, she called Alex.

"Hello?"

"Hey, Alex. It's Maggie."

"Hey, Mags. How are you? Is everything okay?"

"Yeah. Everything is fine. I was just wondering if we could get together tomorrow, rather than wait until Sunday."

"Seriously? Tomorrow would be great. I'd love to see you two days in a row."

"Yeah? I was worried you might have plans. I know it's late notice."

"Nope. I need to do some shopping, but I can do that this afternoon. I'll pick you up in the morning and we'll make a day of it. How would you like to go to the beach?"

"I'd love to. That would be wonderful."

"Great. What time can I pick you up?"

"Say ten?"

"Sounds good. I'll see you then."

Maggie hung up and walked down the hall to her room. She got on her knees and prayed to God again for guidance. She asked Him if it was time for her to leave the Church. She loved Alex and couldn't bear losing her. If happiness with her meant leaving the Church, then Reverend Mother was right. She needed to make some decisions.

Saturday morning, Maggie dressed in her swimsuit with her clothes over it. She packed a bag with underwear and a towel in it. She was ready for her day with Alex. She walked out to the parking lot at ten o'clock to find Alex waiting for her. She climbed into the truck and smiled brightly.

"Hi there."

"Hi, Mags. You ready for a day at the beach?"

"I sure am."

They drove down the freeway until they came to the exit for Avila Beach. They drove the windy road that took them to the placid town. They drove right to the beach, but the parking places were all full so they parked in the public lot a block away. It was a beautiful day for a walk, so neither of them minded.

"It's a bit chilly here," Maggie said.

"Not too chilly, I hope."

"No. It's just cooler than San Luis. But it's early. I'm sure it'll warm up as the day wears on."

They set up their towels on the sand and lay down. It felt good to just relax in the sun.

"Did you want to try the water?" Alex said.

"I'll try it, but I can't guarantee I won't freeze."

They walked to the water's edge, then Maggie walked a little farther, so she was just barely in the water.

"Br. That's cold," she said.

Alex walked out until the water was knee deep on her.

"You're going to freeze," Maggie said.

"Nonsense. The trick is to totally submerge yourself."

With that, she walked a few more steps out and dove underwater. Maggie shivered as she watched. Alex surfaced a few seconds later.

"Aren't you freezing?" Maggie said.

"Au contraire. I feel amazing. Invigorated, even. Come on in. Trust me."

Maggie wasn't sure she did trust Alex but ventured out farther into the water.

"It's cold," she said. "You don't mind now because your whole body is numb."

"Nonsense." Alex walked over to Maggie and took her hands. "Come on. Just a little farther and you'll be able to dive under. It feels amazing. Honest."

Maggie decided to trust Alex and walked out into deeper water. She felt the whole lower half of her body go numb.

"I think you're crazy."

"Nah. Come on."

Maggie walked out a little more and finally did a shallow dive underwater. When she surfaced, she was cold but refreshed.

"It really isn't that bad," she said.

"No. Now, come on. Let's body surf."

The waves at Avila weren't big enough for surfboards, but they were a good size to body surf on. Maggie and Alex tried to catch one after another but kept missing them. They laughed hysterically at their failures. Finally, Maggie managed to catch one and ride it to shore. She jumped up and fought through the waves to get back out to where Alex waited for her.

"That was awesome," she said. "That was so much fun. I want to catch another one."

"Let's do it."

Maggie tried to catch another one but missed it. Alex managed to catch it, though, and Maggie enjoyed watching the wave carry her trim body to shore.

They spent the rest of the morning riding waves until Maggie pleaded hunger. They rinsed off under the public shower and towel dried and dressed, then went to the Custom House for lunch. They each had fish and chips and a Bloody Mary. They sat on the patio and enjoyed the view.

"What a great morning," Maggie said. "This has been fun. Thank you."

"It really has been. And we still have time to go back to my place for a proper shower and some fun before I have to have you back to the convent."

"I do like the sound of that," Maggie said.

They finished lunch and walked back to the truck. Once inside, Alex took Maggie's hand.

"I wish we could hold hands in public," Alex said.

"Is that safe? I mean, two women holding hands? Wouldn't we get stoned or something?"

Alex laughed. It was a deep, easy laugh that caused Maggie's insides to melt.

"No," Alex said. "Not in this day and age. And not around here. Some places maybe, but not around our little town."

"Hm. I guess I haven't really paid attention to that. You know, I only know the Church's teaching on it."

"True."

They got to Alex's house and went directly to the shower to scrub all the salt and sand off themselves and each other. They brought each other to several orgasms in the process.

When they were dry, they collapsed onto Alex's bed. They kissed and stroked each other, enjoying the feel of one another's flesh. Alex rolled Maggie over so she was on her back. She climbed between her legs. Alex buried her face between Maggie's legs and loved her frantically with her tongue. She was rewarded when Maggie called out her name as she climaxed.

Maggie lay still, trying to catch her breath. When she was breathing normally, she ran her hand down Alex's body until she brought it to rest between her legs. She dipped her fingers inside her then pulled them out and plunged them in deeper. She stroked her deep inside and ran her fingertips over all the soft spots she could feel. She found Alex's favorite spot and rubbed it until Alex cried out as she came.

They lay together quietly for a few minutes.

"I'd better get you back to the convent," Alex said.

"Yeah. I suppose you should."

"At least I get to see you tomorrow."

"Yes. We get all day tomorrow after Mass."

"I can't wait," Alex said. "I miss you already."

"You're so sweet." Maggie kissed her hard on her mouth, then made herself stop because they didn't have time to finish what she'd started.

"Come on," Alex said. "Let's get you home before I decide to hold you hostage."

"Oh, if only it were that easy."

"I know. Believe me, I know."

Alex dropped Maggie off at the convent at five minutes before six. Maggie stowed her bag in her room and went to the dining room. She slid into her seat seconds before Reverend Mother said grace.

After dinner, Reverend Mother cornered Maggie.

"Where were you today?" she said.

"At Avila Beach."

"Oh. How was it there?"

"It was beautiful, Reverend Mother. You can really see His glory in the great expanse of ocean."

"Excellent. I'm glad you don't forget to give Him praise at all times."

"Never. I'd never forget that."

"Good."

Maggie excused herself and went to her room. As was the norm, she knelt and prayed. She prayed to God for answers. She said her Our Fathers and Hail Marys. But as usual, she got no answer. She climbed into bed, exhausted and immediately fell asleep.

Sunday morning, Maggie couldn't stop smiling. She went to the dining room for breakfast and, fortunately, Mother Superior wasn't there. Maggie made herself a waffle and ate a yogurt and drank coffee. She felt ready to face the day.

Maggie took her shower and dressed for Mass. She thought she looked good, then chastised herself for her vanity. She didn't need to commit every sin every day. She crossed the garden and took her place in the church.

She sang loudly as she watched the side entrance for Alex's entrance. When she walked in, Maggie's heart skipped a beat. She lost her place in the hymn as her gaze followed Alex from the door to her pew. When Alex smiled at her, she felt her face grow warm. She loved her so much. How could that be wrong?

After Mass and the social hour, they crossed to the convent so Maggie could change. They decided to go to the Firestone Grill for lunch before heading back to Alex's place.

"This is where we first met," Alex said.

"I remember. Did I ever tell you I had a crush on you even before that day?"

"No. Did you really?"

"I did. Big time. And when I realized it was you sitting next to me at the bar, I almost fell off my stool."

Alex laughed.

"I'm glad you didn't. I don't know that we would be where we are today if you had."

"No kidding."

They ate their lunch then drove to Alex's.

"I love your place," Maggie said. "It's so comfortable and so inviting."

"I'm glad you think so. God knows you've been here often enough."

"I love it here."

"Great. Now, speaking of loving..." Alex took Maggie in her arms and kissed her. It was a passionate kiss that spoke of a longing that matched Maggie's.

They walked together to the couch, still kissing, and fell on to it. Maggie lay under Alex and longed for the feel of her flesh against her own. But Alex was in too much of a hurry. She quickly unzipped Maggie's shorts and slid her hand inside. Maggie arched and urged Alex onward. She was on fire and needed Alex's touch.

Alex found Maggie's center and deftly entered her. Maggie squirmed under her, making sure Alex hit all the right spots. When Alex pulled her hand out to rub Maggie's clit, Maggie felt all her energy coalesce deep inside her. Alex continued to press into Maggie's clit, and Maggie felt the energy explode and shoot heat throughout her extremities. She felt her world shatter into a million tiny pieces at the force of the orgasms.

When she could focus again, Alex was standing over her with her hand outstretched.

"Come on," Alex said. "Let's go to bed."

They only made it to the guest room. They were too eager to have each other to go all the way upstairs. It didn't matter. There was a bed and they could enjoy each other just fine there. They tore each other's close off and tossed them on the floor then climbed onto the bed. Alex held Maggie close.

"I love the feel of your skin against mine," she said.

"So do I. Please, Alex. Please take me again."

Alex kissed down Maggie's body until she was between her legs. She threw Maggie's knees over her shoulders and went to work. She licked and sucked all over her until Maggie was crying out again.

"I don't think I've ever come that hard," Maggie said.

"Well, hooray for me," Alex said and then was quiet for a minute. "Maggie, you know I used to be a player, so maybe this isn't a fair question to ask, but how many people have you been with? And have they all been women?"

"Not all women. My first time was with a guy in the dorms. It certainly was nothing to write home about. But after that, they were all women. I've been with three women before you."

"Wow. That's not many."

"Enough to know that I love you and didn't love any of them."

"Oh, I don't doubt your feelings for me," Alex said. "I was just curious."

"Do you have any more questions?" Maggie said before she kissed Alex hard on the mouth.

"Nope. Not a one."

"Excellent answer."

Maggie kissed her again as she moved her hand down between her legs. She found her wet and ready.

"I love how hot and wet you always are for me," Maggie said.

"Always."

"You feel so good."

"So do you, Mags."

Maggie moved her fingers in and out of Alex, slowly at first, but then faster as her need to please her grew. She plunged deep inside her and rubbed her clit with her thumb. The combination caused Alex to issue a guttural moan as she clamped down on Maggie and reached her climax.

"You've got a death grip on my hand," Maggie said.

"Sorry," Alex said. "That was just such a powerful orgasm."

"Oh, don't apologize. It's awesome."

"Good."

Maggie finally managed to extricate her hand and held on to Alex. They snuggled together for a while.

"You want to just stay like this? Or you want to hit the pool?" Alex said.

"I'm sore from fighting with the waves yesterday. So I don't know that I'll swim laps, but I'll certainly sit and watch you."

"That sounds good to me."

They went out into the sunny afternoon and, true to her word, Maggie sat at her usual spot while Alex swam laps. Alex swam over to Maggie afterward.

"I know we ate a decent sized lunch, but I'm hungry again. Would you mind if I started dinner?"

"Not at all."

They ate their dinner then went back to the bedroom where they loved each other for several more hours. They were both completely spent when Alex broke the mood.

"Hey, Mags. I need to get you back to the convent. I don't want you to miss curfew."

"Yeah. I know. I just hate leaving you. Especially since I won't see you again until Saturday."

"Oh, yeah?" Alex said. "We're going to hang out Saturday again?"

"You'd better believe it."

"Right on."

Alex held Maggie's hand as they drove back to the convent. Once they parked, Maggie pulled her hand away.

"I hate letting go of you," Alex said.

"I know, but we need to be careful."

"I know."

They said their good nights and Maggie let herself into her room where she fell asleep feeling happier than ever.

Chapter Nineteen

Maggie threw herself into her work the following week. She spent long hours in the classroom, either grading homework or working on her plans for the next day. She went out of her way to avoid Reverend Mother except at dinners, and it worked.

Friday night after dinner, Maggie dropped to her knees and once again asked God for guidance. She felt like she was caught between two worlds and just wanted to know which way to go. Still having received no answers, Maggie went to bed.

Maggie and Alex were trapped. Wherever they were was dark and dismal. Even the reds and oranges reflected off the walls couldn't bring light to the darkness. And it stunk. The smell of sulfur assaulted her nostrils.

It was also hot. Maggie was hotter than she'd ever been in her life. She and Alex tried to cling to each other for comfort, but their skin burned at the contact.

And the sounds were horrifying. Screams of tortured souls reverberated off the walls. Maggie opened her mouth to scream, but no sound came out. She was terrified, more afraid than she'd ever been. She had a sinking feeling she knew where she was and was frightened that she'd never get out.

Then there was a disturbance from up above. Two men were shouting at each other. And then there was light above them, a white light that framed the face of a kindly looking older gentleman. He had a long white beard, and the light seemed a part of him. He reached his hand down for hers. At first, she shied away, fearing it would burn her.

"Take it," he said.

She took his hand, and it was cool and comforting.

"Promise me you'll stay with me always," he said. "And I'll get you both out."

"I promise," Maggie said. "I promise. I'll stay with you forever."

He lifted Maggie and Alex out of there and set them gently on the ground.

"Don't forget your promise," he said. "I won't save you again."

Maggie woke in a cold sweat. If she'd been looking for an answer, she certainly found one there. God had spoken to her. He wanted her to devote her life to Him. She would have to break it off with Alex. The idea made her stomach churn, but she knew it was the right thing to do. The only thing to do.

She checked her clock. It was three forty-five in the morning. She knew she was wide-awake and that she wouldn't sleep any more that night. She climbed out of bed and knelt at her kneeler. She promised God she would break up with Alex and would only serve Him from now on. She promised to go to confession and confess her sins and begin her vows anew.

She prayed for several hours, then got up and took her shower. She dressed in shorts and a T-shirt and went to the dining room for breakfast. She didn't have much of an appetite but made herself eat a yogurt and some fruit. She drank gallons of coffee to cure the sleepiness that threatened to take over.

When it was ten o'clock, she walked out to the parking lot to meet Alex. Her stomach was in knots, but she knew what she had to do.

"Hey, Mags," Alex said. "What do you want to do today?"

"Let's start by getting coffee somewhere."

"Okay. Is everything okay with you?"

"Alex, we need to talk."

"Oh, shit. I don't like the sound of that."

"Let's just get some coffee, okay?"

"If that's what you want, then sure."

They pulled into a coffee shop.

"Do you want something to eat?" Alex said.

"I'm not hungry."

"Yeah. Suddenly, I have no appetite, either."

They got their coffees and sat on the patio out front.

"So, what do we need to talk about?" Alex said.

"Alex, you know I've been praying for guidance, right? For God to tell me what I need to do."

"Yeah. And?"

"He came to me in a dream last night. He told me I could only be saved if I served only Him."

"What?"

Maggie told her about the dream, about how horrible it was. Tears flowed down her cheeks as she recounted it.

"Sh. It's okay. It was just a dream," Alex said.

"No. I don't think it was."

"Okay. No. Maybe not. Maybe it was a message from God. I don't mean to belittle it. I just mean the dream is over now and you're okay."

"But I'm having to break up with the love of my life."

"Yeah. Not my idea of a good time, either. But I'll honor your request, Maggie. We both knew it might come to this someday. And now it has. We had a good run, but I will accept it's over if that's what I need to do."

"I'm so sorry, Alex," Maggie said. "And thank you for taking it so well."

"Well, inside, my heart is breaking, but I have to understand. You were committed to the Church long before you met me. And if that's where you need to make your lifelong commitment rather than with me, I have to concede to that."

"You're so wonderful. I'm going to miss you so much."

"So, I guess staying friends is out of the question?"

"I don't know, Alex. I don't know that I'm strong enough to be your friend."

"I get that," Alex said. "I'll still see you at Mass and such."

"I suppose you will."

"Yeah."

They sat in an awkward, prolonged silence.

"So," Alex said. "I suppose I should take you back to the convent?"

"Yes, please."

"I'm going to miss you, Mags."

"I'll miss you, too. But it's what I need to do."

"I understand."

Alex gave Maggie's hand a squeeze before she got out of the truck. Maggie fought tears as she cut through the garden to her room. She threw herself on the bed and let the tears flow. She was sobbing when she heard a knock on the door. She wiped her eyes and opened the door. There stood Reverend Mother.

"Maggie? Child, what's wrong? You look horrible. I heard you crying all the way out in the hall."

"I'm sorry. Yes, ma'am. I'm fine. Or will be. Please. Don't worry about me."

"Ah, but I do. I rather expected you to be spending the day with Ms. Foster."

"Not today."

"Do you want to talk about it?"

"No, ma'am. Thank you, though."

"Okay then. I'll leave you be. My door is always open as you know if you need a shoulder to cry on or an ear to talk to."

"Thank you. I appreciate that."

"It's almost time for lunch. Won't you join me? I'll meet you there in an hour."

Maggie wasn't sure she'd be ready to eat anything in an hour but agreed anyway.

"Yes, ma'am. I'll meet you there."

"Thank you, my dear. Now, get it all out of your system and I'll see you soon."

Maggie sat at her desk and buried her face in her hands. How could she get it all out of her system? She felt like she had a giant hole in her heart. But she knew this was what God wanted. He'd made it perfectly clear. She'd been asking Him for guidance, and He'd shown her the way. If only it didn't have to hurt so desperately.

As lunchtime approached, Maggie went to the restroom and washed her face. She still had splotches all over it and her eyes were puffy, but at least she'd stopped crying nonstop. She just hoped she could hold it together during lunch.

Reverend Mother was at the sandwich bar when Maggie walked in. Maggie got in line and made herself a ham sandwich and grabbed a Diet Pepsi. She sat down across from Reverend Mother at an otherwise empty table.

"How are you feeling, Maggie?" Mother Superior said.

"I'll be okay. It's just going to take some time."

"I'm sure you will be. Whatever rough patch you're going through, make sure you pray for guidance. He's always listening to our prayers."

"Yes, ma'am."

"May I ask, does this have anything to do with Ms. Foster? Did she hurt you?"

"No, ma'am. She didn't hurt me."

Maggie longed to tell Reverend Mother about her dream, but if she did, she'd be admitting to her affair with Alex. And she couldn't bring herself to do that.

"Reverend Mother?" she said. "May I borrow your car this afternoon?"

"Certainly. Can you tell me why?"

"There's just someplace I have to go. I'd rather not say where."

"I don't like all this secrecy, but I will trust you. You're a wonderful nun and a great woman, Maggie. You may borrow my car."

"Thank you, Reverend Mother."

At four thirty, Maggie took Reverend Mother's car to the other Catholic Church in town. She knew they didn't have traditional confessionals and that she'd have to sit face-to-face with the priest to confess her sins, but it was better for her than to confess to Father Bremer. She couldn't deal with that.

When it was her turn, she walked into the small room.

"Sister Mary Margaret, isn't it?" The priest said. "Aren't you a teacher down at Old Mission?"

"I am."

"And you're here to say your confession?"

"I am."

"You may begin."

"Bless me, Father, for I have sinned."

"And how long has it been since your last confession?"

"It's been several months."

"And what do you wish to confess to today?"

"Father," Maggie said. "I've broken one of my vows."

"That's very serious indeed."

"Yes, sir. But I won't do it again. I promise."

"Which vow did you break, Sister?"

"I broke my vow of chastity."

"Ah, yes. That's a hard one to uphold. And how will you avoid the temptation in the future?"

"I've removed the temptation from my life."

"Smart. And you believe you are strong enough to keep it removed?"

"I do."

"Very well. Are there any other sins you'd like to confess?"

Maggie thought of all the times she was with Alex and called God's name.

"I've also used God's name in vain."

"And you are promising me now you'll avoid the occurrence to do that again?"

"I promise."

"Very well, my child. I absolve you from your sins. In the name of the Father, the Son, and the Holy Spirit. For your penance, I order you to say five Our Fathers and ten Hail Marys. Go now in peace."

Maggie crossed herself. She wanted to hug the priest, she felt so much better. But she refrained.

"Thank you, Father," she said. She went out into the church and said her prayers. When she was through, she drove back to the convent. She walked down the hall and ran into Reverend Mother.

"Will you still be needing my car, Maggie?" Reverend Mother said.

"I've already borrowed it. It's back in its usual spot. Thank you again for letting me use it."

"No problem."

Maggie went to her room and knelt down. She thanked God for showing her the way, even though the way was painful. She asked him for strength to get through the agony. And the ability to avoid Alex at all costs.

She got up and went down the hall to dinner. After dinner, Reverend Mother approached her.

"Are you ready to tell me where you went this afternoon?"

Maggie was feeling much better about life by then. She felt lighter than she had earlier.

"I went to confession, Reverend Mother. I wasn't comfortable confessing to Father Bremer, so I went to Nativity and went to confession there."

"Hm. I wondered as much. Are you ready to talk to me about it?"

"I don't know."

"I think it's important that you do. You need to talk to me about what's bothering you."

"Maybe at some point, but I don't know that I'm ready."

"It's important that you not keep secrets from me," Reverend Mother said. "Why don't we go to my office."

It was clear she wasn't taking no for an answer, so Maggie drew a deep breath and followed her down the hall. Once in her office, Reverend Mother closed the door behind Maggie.

"Please, sit down," she said.

Maggie sat on one side of the old desk, and Reverend Mother took her place behind it. Maggie sat quietly looking at her hands.

"Now, Maggie. You understand why I need to know what's happening, right?"

"No, ma'am."

"I know you went to confession. Did you do your penance?"

"Yes, ma'am.

"Do you feel absolved?"

"Yes, ma'am."

"Good. That's important. Now, will you please tell me what was so important you couldn't tell Father Bremer?"

"I thought confession was between me and the priest," Maggie said.

"In most cases, it is. But if it's something more than the usual transgressions, I might need to weigh in on things."

Maggie sat silently. She fought back tears. She didn't want to admit to Mother Superior that she'd been right the whole time. She felt like a failure as a nun. But she'd been absolved and was free to go back to being the good nun she'd been before.

"Maggie? Please. Say something."

"You were right," Maggie said. The tears flowed silently down her cheeks. "I was having an affair with Alex."

"I thought as much," Reverend Mother said softly. "And who called it off?"

"I did."

Maggie told Reverend Mother about the dream she'd had the previous night.

"Oh, my. That would have frightened me, too," Reverend Mother said. "The Lord works in mysterious ways."

"Yes, ma'am He does. I woke up from the dream and knew what He wanted me to do. Oh, Reverend Mother, I'd been praying so hard for guidance and He'd never shown me any. I didn't know if He wanted me to pursue my relationship with her or remain a nun. But the dream made it pretty clear."

"I'd say."

They sat in silence for a few more minutes.

"So," Reverend Mother said. "You broke up with her. That must have been hard."

"Yes and no. It hurts, Reverend Mother. I feel like a part of me is missing. But I know it was the right thing to do. And she took it very well. Like she said, we'd both known it might come to this. And it did, so she was okay with it."

"Did you love her?"

"Yes."

"I see. Do you still?"

"It's not that easy to turn off an emotion, Reverend Mother."

"No. I know that. How can you be sure you won't transgress?"

"I know she loves me, so I know she'll respect my need not to see her again. And I know I won't seek her out. We've gone our separate ways. I've accepted that."

"Okay. Well, now I have to say this. You know how grave an offense it is to break your vows."

"Yes, ma'am. But I went to confession. I'm all set now."

"But it's up to me to decide whether this was a one-time infraction or if I believe it will be a problem in the future. That's why I needed you to talk to me."

"Please, Reverend Mother. It was a one-time thing. I fell in love. I will go out of my way to make sure it doesn't happen again."

"I believe you, my child. Now, go in peace."

"Thank you. I'll see you tomorrow."

"Sounds good."

Maggie went to bed that night feeling torn. She felt light, resolved, and right walking on God's path again. But she missed Alex. So much so that she cried herself to sleep.

CHAPTER TWENTY

Maggie was up early the next morning. She ate breakfast at six thirty, then showered and dressed. Determined not to see Alex, she opted to go to the eight thirty Mass. She took her place in the pews and was singing the processional hymn when she saw her walk in. What was she doing there? Clearly, she'd had the same idea as Maggie. She'd come to the early Mass to avoid her. When their gazes met across the church, Alex turned and left. Maggie felt an overwhelming sense of relief. She didn't know what she'd have said to her. She wasn't all that great at small talk except at the coffee and doughnut social. Small talk with an ex would have killed her, she was sure.

Her mind was wandering, though, and that was something she'd sworn against. She'd promised herself to focus on God and God only. She turned her attention to the Mass. She watched with deep faith as the Host was consecrated. She took her turn in line, and when she received the Holy Communion, she was filled with a peace she hadn't known in far too long.

After Mass, Maggie changed her clothes and worked in the garden. Several parishioners had donated annuals that needed to be planted. She was happy to do it. She prayed as she planted, thanking God for all He had bestowed upon her. It was a beautiful summer day, not too hot. It was a perfect day to be in the sun. She worked until her knees and back were too sore to go on. She got up and went inside.

Maggie took another shower and put on clean clothes. She wandered into town for dinner. She stopped at a sandwich shop and ate at a sidewalk table. She loved watching the people milling about. Summer was such a fun time in her town. The students were mostly all gone, but the tourists more than made up for their absence. She took a bite of her sandwich when she heard her voice.

"Hello, Maggie. I didn't expect to see you here."

Maggie turned to see Alex standing over her. What should she do? She wanted to run away, to avoid her completely, but, clearly, it was too late.

"Would you care to join me?"

"If you think that would be a good idea."

"Why not? We're just two people who happened to buy sandwiches at the same stop. That is what happened, right? This is a chance meeting?"

"Of course. I'm not stalking you if that's what you mean."

"I'm sorry. That did sound kind of harsh. Please. Sit down."

Alex sat across the table from her. Maggie searched for something to say.

"So, I take it you chose to go to eleven o'clock Mass instead of eight thirty this morning?"

"Yeah. Seeing you there, well, I just hadn't planned on seeing you and it hurt too much. I didn't mean to be rude."

"You weren't rude. I understood completely. And you're okay sitting with me now? It doesn't hurt too much?"

"Does it hurt you?"

"Not to sound childish, but I asked you first."

Alex laughed. The sound warmed Maggie all over. Careful, she warned herself. Don't fall again.

"No. I mean, yeah, to a degree, but we can't be avoiding each other all the time. Our paths are bound to cross. It's a small town and we go to the same church."

"True. I get what you're saying. It makes total sense."

They sat eating their sandwiches when someone else walked up.

"Good evening, ladies."

Maggie looked up to see Reverend Mother staring down at her. She swallowed hard. She knew how it must look, but it wasn't that way.

"Hello, Reverend Mother," Maggie said. "We just ran into each other here and are grabbing a bite. Would you care to join us?"

"No, thank you. I just had my dinner. I'll be getting back to the convent now. Maggie, I'd like to see you in my office in an hour."

"Yes, ma'am."

Maggie and Alex finished their dinners.

"Do you want a lift back to the convent?" Alex said.

"No, thanks. It's a lovely evening, and it's not much of a walk."

"Okay. If you're sure."

"I'm sure."

They stood in awkward silence.

"So, um, Maggie?"

"Yeah?"

"You think we'll both be able to go to the same Mass? You think we can handle it?"

"I think so. We're both adults. Life will go on."

"Yes, it will. Well, it was good seeing you."

"You, too."

"Good night."

"Good night."

Maggie walked the short distance back to the convent and went to her room. She sat there saying the Rosary while she waited for the time to meet with Reverend Mother. When the time arrived, she dragged herself down the hall, filled with dread at the upcoming meeting.

Reverend Mother looked up when Maggie entered the room.

"Maggie. Please, sit down."

Reverend Mother walked over and closed the door then took her place behind her desk. She simply stared at Maggie, who stared at her hands.

"Do you want to explain to me what I saw this evening?"

"It was an honest running into one another. I promise. It wasn't planned."

"Maggie, you mustn't lie to me."

"I'm not lying. I got a sandwich and was sitting there minding my own business when she walked up. I swear it was nothing more."

"I have a hard time believing that."

"Reverend Mother, I made a mistake. I know that. And I've confessed my sins. I want nothing more than to go back to my normal life as a normal nun."

"You're much more than a normal nun, which is why I'm so concerned."

"You've nothing to be concerned about. I assure you. It went down exactly as I'm telling you. She walked over and said hello and I invited her to join me. Maybe that wasn't the best idea, but I'm glad it happened. We talked about how hard it would be to avoid one another and figured seeing each other like that was the first step in being able to be in the same space without freaking out."

"I noticed you went to the early Mass today. Was that to avoid seeing her?"

"Yes. Unfortunately, she went to the same Mass with the same idea."

"And?"

"And as soon as she saw me, she left."

"She did?"

"Yes, ma'am. And then I focused solely on the Mass."

"Maggie. I need you to be completely honest with me here. Are you one hundred percent over Alex Foster?"

"Reverend Mother, it will be a process. As I said yesterday, it's not easy to switch an emotion like love off. But you can rest assured that I have no interest in her in any way other than as another parishioner. I'm not going to pursue her, and I believe she respects me too much to pursue me. We agreed that we'll be okay seeing each other at Mass and other functions. It won't be easy at first. I know this. But I believe we'll get to a comfortable place, and I believe tonight was the first step."

"Okay, Maggie. I'm going to believe you, but I think it would be in your best interest to further avoid her in the near future."

"But, Reverend Mother, I like the eleven o'clock Mass. I like the social afterward. I like talking to the parishioners. I don't want to continue to go to the eight thirty Mass."

"And you think she'll go to the eleven o'clock Mass?"

"I do."

"Well, there's nothing wrong with being at the same Mass. As long as she's not distracting you from the service."

"She won't."

"And I don't recall seeing her at the social until you two started hanging out, is that right?" Reverend Mother said.

"That's correct. I doubt she'll be going to them now."

"I hope not. If she does, I'd better not see you hanging out with her and her alone."

"You won't." Maggie was getting exasperated. "What do I need to say to prove to you I'm serious about my vows and won't be making the same mistake again?"

"Maggie, the first step, I would think, would be to avoid the temptation altogether. That's what I'm trying to get at here."

"Yes, ma'am. I understand that. And I won't allow myself to be tempted again. I know I'm stronger than this."

"Ah, but you thought you were before, too, didn't you?"

"I knew I was weak, Reverend Mother. I've always been weak, but now I know I'm strong. I'm rededicated. God gave me a message, and I'm taking it to heart."

"Okay, Maggie," Reverend Mother said. "If you're sure."

"I am."

"I have to trust you. But know I'll be keeping my eye on you. Both to help keep you from slipping and to see how you handle the temptation. I can't have a scandal rocking this convent. Not on my watch."

"No, ma'am. I wouldn't do that to you."

"You could have."

"But I didn't."

"No," Reverend Mother said. "But I was so afraid it was coming. I'm glad you came to your senses before it came to that."

"Me, too."

"Okay, Maggie. Now that you and I have talked about it a couple of times, I hope you'll be comfortable coming to see me if you're ever feeling tempted or just need to talk."

"Thank you. Reverend Mother. I appreciate that."

"Good night, Maggie."

"Good night."

Maggie woke the next morning, had some breakfast, and grabbed a sack lunch. Then she was off to school. The day passed quickly, and after, she stayed and graded the kids' schoolwork. It was a good day, and she felt good when she went back to the convent for dinner.

Reverend Mother said grace, then took her plate and sat next to Maggie.

"Hello, Maggie. How was your day?"

"It was great, Reverend Mother. How was yours?"

"Oh, mine was interesting. One of the older kids got sent to my office. I always hate when that happens. I have to scare the living daylights out of them. It's fun in some sort of sadistic way, but I do feel sorry for the poor kids."

Maggie had to laugh. She had to admit that she'd been terrified of Reverend Mother until recently when she'd taken the time to talk to Maggie about what she'd been going through. Now, she felt a special bond with her. She realized Reverend Mother was as human as the rest of them.

"I feel sorry for the kids, too," Maggie said. "But not so much that I won't send them to see you if they continuously misbehave."

"Very good. That's one of the things I'm here for."

"And you're so good at it."

"Why, thank you. I think."

They laughed together and continued to eat.

"So, you really had a good day?" Reverend Mother said.

"Yeah. I lost myself in my teaching and then stayed late at school grading their work. It was a really good day."

"So, you're feeling okay, then? That's a good thing. That makes me happy."

"Yes, ma'am. I'm dreading the weekend a little bit, but I'll get through. I know I will."

"Yes. The weekend will be hardest for you. Just make extra time to pray."

"Yes, ma'am. I will."

The rest of the week passed easily for Maggie. Nights were hard as she lay in bed thinking of Alex. She tried to shut her mind off, but she couldn't help thinking of her, wondering what she was doing. She could picture her with a glass of wine on her patio. Or swimming laps in her pool. It was hard, but she got through them. Then Saturday arrived.

Maggie woke with a longing she hadn't felt in the week since she'd left Alex. She woke with her hands on her breasts and quickly moved them to her sides. She didn't need to think like that. And she wouldn't give in to self-pleasure. That, too, was a sin, though, obviously not as harsh of one as breaking her vows. Still, she was disgusted with herself.

She got out of bed and went down the hall to take her shower. Several nuns were already there, so Maggie waited her turn with a younger nun, Sister Josephine Michael, Jo for short.

"How have you been, Maggie?" Jo said.

"I've been good, Jo. How about you?"

"Not bad. It just seems I've seen you and Reverend Mother together a lot lately and I wanted to make sure you're not in some kind of trouble."

"Oh, no. I'm fine. Thanks for checking, though."

"Sure. If you do get into trouble, you know I'm a good listener."

"I appreciate that, but I'm fine. Really."

A shower opened and Jo stepped into the stall. Maggie breathed a sigh of relief. She didn't want to be talking to anyone about what she and Reverend Mother had talked about. She'd take that secret to her grave.

She finally got a chance to shower and did so, feeling better to have the warm water wash over her. She scrubbed away all the impure thoughts she'd had that morning. Finally clean, she dried, dressed, and went back to her room to put her night clothes away.

Next, it was time for breakfast. She was starving so made a waffle, had some yogurt and fruit, and a cup of coffee. She sat in quiet solitude to eat before contemplating what to do with her day. She knew she'd work in the garden. She just didn't know how much she had to do.

"May I join you?" She looked up and saw Reverend Mother standing there. As much as she appreciated all Reverend Mother was trying to do and be for her, she sometimes wished she'd just leave her alone.

"Sure," she said.

"How are you this morning?"

"I'm okay. I got off to a rough start, but I'm okay now."

"A rough start? How so?" Reverend Mother said.

"I woke up with Alex on my mind. It was shocking. But I took my shower and came here to get food. I'll be fine."

"What are your plans for the day?"

"I plan to work in the garden. I want to pull some more weeds and get the rest of those flowers planted."

"Would you like some company?"

Company? Reverend Mother's company? That was the last thing she wanted.

"You're welcome to join me if you want," Maggie said. "But I do like the solitude of working out there. I spend most of my time praying."

"Okay. As long as you're praying and not letting your mind wander to Ms. Foster."

"No, ma'am. I won't allow that to happen."

"Very good."

Maggie cleared her place and went out to the garden. She spent all day working and was good and sore and took another shower before dinner. After dinner, she went to her room to pray until she could barely keep her eyes open. But when she climbed into bed, she was hit with the realization that she would see Alex the next morning and she wasn't sure she'd be ready for that.

Chapter Twenty-one

Maggie was up earlier than she'd planned the next morning. She'd hoped to sleep in so her mind wouldn't work overtime, but no such luck. She was up by seven. She showered, had a quick breakfast, and had too much time to kill before Mass. She knelt and prayed for strength to get through the day and asked God to allow her to focus on the Mass and not on Alex.

Her stomach was in knots at the prospect of seeing Alex. Even though they'd had a nice chat the other evening, she still was on edge. She walked to the church early and knelt there to pray. When it was time to sing, she stood and sang, feeling filled with a combination of God and dread. She pushed the dread deep inside her and sang to celebrate God. She was completely engrossed in His Holiness when she saw Alex enter. Dang it. Why hadn't she sat somewhere where she couldn't see her? But she hadn't, and there she was. She watched her genuflect and enter her pew. When she stood still, their gazes met, and Alex smiled at her. Maggie smiled back, lost in the moment. Then, she brought herself back to what was important and focused on the Mass.

When Mass was over, Maggie went to the hall for coffee and doughnuts.

"How are you?" Alex said.

"What? Why are you here?"

"I thought we agreed not to be awkward around each other. You knew you'd run into me."

"I didn't think you'd be here," Maggie said. "I mean, you never used to go to socials."

"No, but then I started to, and now I enjoy them. I'm sorry. I didn't mean to upset you."

Maggie was frustrated that her emotions were that obvious.

"You didn't upset me," she lied. "You simply surprised me is all."

"Okay, good. Then I don't feel as bad."

Reverend Mother was upon them before Maggie had even seen her in the hall.

"Sister, shouldn't you be mingling?" she said.

"Yes, ma'am." She turned to Alex. "Excuse me."

Maggie wandered through the hall, relieved to have some space between herself and Alex. The draw was still there, the desire too close to the surface to be too close to her. She was grateful Reverend Mother had stepped in but feared it would mean another talking to.

She made her way through the parishioners talking to them about what they'd been doing on their summer vacations and visiting with the few who were going to summer school. When she had circled back to the doughnut table, Alex was gone. She breathed a sigh of relief until she saw her across the room talking to a small group of people.

Why did it have to be so hard? They'd had dinner the week before and it was fine. So, what was she freaking over now? She took a deep calming breath and helped herself to another doughnut. Reverend Mother approached her.

"Are you okay?" she said.

"Yes. Fine."

"I'll want to talk to you after this."

"Yes, ma'am. I thought you would. But it was all innocent, I assure you."

"Sh. Now is not the time or the place. I'll see you in my office when the social is over."

"Yes, ma'am."

Maggie took another cup of coffee and made another sweep of the room, always careful not to be near Alex. When the parishioners filed out, Maggie helped the other nuns get things put away. She left the building and was surprised to find Alex waiting for her out front.

"Hey, Maggie."

Maggie looked around frantically but saw no escape.

"Hi, Alex. What's up?"

"You okay? Worried that your mother superior is going to hound us again?"

"No. I'm fine." Maggie smiled.

"Good. So I don't suppose you'd want to grab a bite to eat, would you?"

"Thanks, but no thanks. I have to meet with Reverend Mother."

"Mags, you didn't tell her about us, did you?"

"Actually, I did."

Alex exhaled slowly.

"Why, may I ask?" she said.

"Alex, she knew. She'd always known. And when a nun breaks her vows, it's customary for the mother superior to decide whether it's likely to happen again. You know, to decide if the nun needs to leave the convent."

Alex's eyebrows shot up.

"And? What did she decide?"

"That it was a one-time indiscretion."

"Maggie, it was more than once."

"You know what I mean. That it's not likely I'm going to run off and have another affair."

"I should hope not."

"No. I won't."

"Okay," Alex said. "If your mother superior is waiting for you, I won't keep you. I sure do miss you, though."

"I miss you, too. I'd be a liar if I said I didn't. But I can't go back. I have to move forward and do God's work."

"I understand. I'll see you around, Maggie."

"See ya."

Maggie hurried to the convent and down the hall to Reverend Mother's office.

"What took you so long?"

"Alex, er, Ms. Foster, was waiting for me in the parking lot."

"Maggie. I don't think it's wise for you to be around her. At least not yet."

"I didn't expect to see her at the social, Reverend Mother."

"And that was quite apparent by your reaction. Anyone watching you two would have known something was up."

"Fortunately, it's doubtful anyone was watching us."

"Why do you say that, my child? You're a well-known, well-loved nun here. People pay attention to you. I'm sure there are those who come to the socials just to visit with you. People watch you. They see you. And I'm concerned that that little altercation didn't go unnoticed."

"Oh, Reverend Mother, please don't say that. And it wasn't an altercation even."

"It was from where I stood," Reverend Mother said.

"I was just surprised to see her there. That was all."

"Well, it looked hostile to me, which is why I intervened. That, and I don't want you led into temptation again."

"I won't be. Believe me. My faith and commitment to my vows have never been stronger."

"I'm happy to hear that. Still, I think you should avoid her for a while. I know you like eleven o'clock Mass, but maybe you should go to eight thirty for a while."

"But, Reverend Mother, I really do enjoy the social. I like visiting with the parishioners."

"That includes Ms. Foster, and I don't think you should be visiting with her. Not yet."

"When, then?"

"I don't know. Just give it some time. Please."

"Yes, ma'am."

"Thank you. Now get out there and enjoy this beautiful weather. I noticed some new weeds cropping up over by the irises. That should keep you busy for a while."

"Yes, ma'am."

"Would you like to have dinner again tonight, Maggie? That way I don't have to worry about you running into Ms. Foster, and neither of us has to eat alone."

Maggie no more wanted to have dinner with Reverend Mother than she wanted to get back together with Alex, but she had a feeling it was an order more than a request.

"That sounds great. Thank you," she said.

"Wonderful. I'll be by your room at six to get you."

"Thanks again. I'd better go tend to those weeds."

Maggie went to work in the garden and lost herself in it. She checked her watch and saw that it was already five thirty. She hurried inside to shower and get ready for Reverend Mother. She was sitting at her desk when Reverend Mother knocked at precisely six o'clock.

Maggie was dressed in a skirt and blouse since she had no idea where Reverend Mother would want to go to dinner and she thought she'd better look nice.

"Where are we going tonight?" Maggie said.

"I thought we'd try Novo. I've heard good things about it."

"Oh, so have I. Are you sure it's not too spendy?"

"You let me worry about that, my child. I'm buying, after all."

They drove to the little restaurant and took their seats on the patio overlooking the creek. It was a pleasant spot, nice and quiet, and Maggie thought she'd probably like to come back.

"So, what's the occasion?" Maggie said.

"I told you. I didn't want either of us to have to eat alone."

"And you want to make sure I'm not meeting Alex for dinner."

"I'll admit that did cross my mind," Reverend Mother said.

"So, you don't believe me that my running into her last weekend was strictly by chance?"

"Not particularly."

"I thought we agreed to be honest with each other. I thought I promised you my honesty so you could help me get through this. And yet, the first chance you have to trust me, you don't."

"Put yourself in my place, Maggie. The day after you tell me you've broken up I see you two having dinner together. What would you have thought?"

"I get why you thought that, but then I told you what happened. I'm hurt you don't believe me."

"Oh, child," Reverend Mother said. "I'm not trying to hurt you. I'm trying to help you. You know that line from The Lord's Prayer, 'lead us not into temptation'? Sometimes you need a little help to avoid it. That's where I come in."

"And I appreciate it, Mother Superior. But I have no desire to be tempted again."

"Did you have the desire to be tempted at the beginning of your relationship with her?"

That was a hard question. She'd already been tempted by Alex even before she'd met her. She thought back to that Sunday months ago when she had touched herself to thoughts of Alex. That was the morning of that fateful day. So had she wanted to be tempted? Yes, she knew she had.

"Maggie?" Reverend Mother said. "Are you with me?"

"If I'm honest, and you want me to be honest, I was tempted by Alex before we started seeing each other. Did I *want* to be tempted by her? I'd say no. But was I? Yes. Definitely."

"Hm. So you do have a problem with attractions of the flesh." It was a statement, not a question.

"I don't think so. I had a problem being attracted to her, yes. But overall, that's not a problem for me."

"It will take some convincing on your part for me to believe this. And you'll convince me with actions, not words."

Their food was served and they ate in an uncomfortable silence for a few minutes.

"Listen, Maggie," Reverend Mother said. "I don't mean to be too hard on you. I just don't want to lose you. I've said it before, but it bears repeating. You're a great nun. You're a natural. The fact that you broke your vows only proves you're human. And you'll need to work on that. And prove to me that your heart belongs to our Lord."

"I will. You'll see. I'll work doubly hard to show our Lord the praise He deserves."

"Excellent, my child. That's what I need to see. You'll do it. And then I'll be able to rest easy."

They finished their dinner and drove back to the convent. They parted ways at Maggie's room.

"Remember what I said," Reverend Mother said. "Eight thirty Mass only for a while."

"Yes, ma'am. Good night. And thank you for dinner."

"You're welcome. Good night."

Maggie dropped to her knees as soon as her door was closed and prayed. She thanked God for her newfound devotion and asked Him for strength to show Reverend Mother she couldn't be distracted any more. Through with her prayers, she fell into an easy sleep.

She woke up the next morning and went through her usual morning routine. She went to work and taught her classes. She taught English in summer school, rather than her usual elementary class. Several kids needed extended help in the subject, and since it was her specialty, she taught the classes. The kids ranged in grade from six through nine.

She worked hard with each grade group, helping each child as needed. When class was over, she sat at her desk and reviewed their schoolwork. She then worked on her lesson plan for the next day. It was five thirty when she left her classroom and headed back to the convent.

Maggie changed into comfortable clothes and headed down the hall to dinner. She took her seat across a table from Jo and waited for Reverend Mother to say grace. Jo and Maggie dug into their dinners.

"So, Maggie," Jo said, "I've been meaning to ask you how you got so tan this summer."

"I spent a lot of time at a pool."

"Really? How nice. How'd you manage that?"

Maggie felt a knot in her stomach. She fought tears. She wasn't ready to talk about Alex. She took a deep breath.

"One of the parishioners has a pool. I was hanging out there for a while on Sundays."

"Oh, is that the same woman who took you to Italy?"

"Yep."

"You're so lucky. I'd love to go to Europe, Italy especially."

Maggie was struggling not to cry, but the memories of the trip, of the good times she'd shared with Alex, were in the forefront of her mind.

"Will you excuse me?"

Maggie went to the restroom to splash water on her face and blow her nose. She turned to see Reverend Mother standing there.

"Are you okay, Maggie?" she said.

"I'm fine. Fine."

"You don't look fine. What's going on?"

"Jo started talking about Italy and my trip, and I got all filled with memories and wanted to cry so I came in here for some privacy."

"Well, you can have all the privacy you want, except you have to deal with me. I'm sorry to interrupt, but I'm worried about you."

"I'll be okay. We both knew this would be a process. I'm working through it."

"Okay. Well, you look better. Let's get back to the dining room."

Maggie sat back down across from Jo.

"What was the best part of Italy?" Jo said.

Making love with Alex all night, she thought.

"The Vatican. Definitely the Vatican," she said.

"Oh, I bet." She shook her head. "I just can't even imagine how awesome it must have been."

"Yeah. Every church we went to was amazing. The artwork, the detail. It was all simply stunning."

"You're really lucky," Jo said.

"I am indeed. I am blessed."

"Amen to that."

CHAPTER TWENTY-TWO

A month went by, and Maggie had thrown herself into her work and her prayers. She'd only attended eight thirty Mass and felt she was ready to go to eleven o'clock Mass again. She went to Reverend Mother's office.

"Well, hello, Maggie." Reverend Mother looked up from her work. "To what do I owe this visit?"

"I need to talk to you."

"What about?"

"Reverend Mother, I miss eleven o'clock Mass. And school will be starting soon, so I think it's important I be seen at the socials to interact with current and any potential new students. I think I'm ready. May I please have your permission?"

"Maggie. You've been doing so well. I'd hate to see you falter. But you make some good points. Promise me you'll avoid Ms. Foster?"

"I'll do my best."

"Very well then. But I'll be watching you."

"Yes, ma'am."

The following Sunday, Maggie slept in a little, then got up and showered and made her way to the church. She knelt in the front pew of Alex's section. Her back was to the door Alex would come in, so she wouldn't have to see her. Maggie said her prayers, then rose as the priest entered.

She focused on the Mass and was filled with a sense of peace when she received Holy Communion. As she turned away from the priest, she saw Alex in line a few people behind her. Alex gave a little smile which Maggie returned.

Back in her spot, Maggie knelt and reflected on the Holy Sacrament and thanked God for coming into her. And she asked Him to allow her to serve Him for many years to come. After Mass, she crossed over to the parish hall for the coffee and doughnut social.

She had just grabbed a cup of coffee when Alex approached her.

"It's nice to see you again," she said. "Where have you been?"

"I've been going to eight thirty Mass."

She watched as Alex's face fell.

"Oh."

"Mother Superior's orders," Maggie said.

"Oh. I see. But you're back now?"

"Yes. We both believe enough time has passed and I should be here at the socials."

"Well, I'll let you mingle. It's good to see you, though."

Maggie wanted to say how horrible it was to see Alex, how much it pained her, how incredibly handsome she looked, how much she missed her. But she said none of those things.

"Good seeing you, too," she said.

Maggie made her way through the crowd. Reverend Mother signaled to her from across the room. She cringed inwardly. She didn't want a speech just because she'd spent a few minutes talking to Alex. But she couldn't ignore her. She crossed to where Reverend Mother stood with a family of three.

"Sister Mary Margaret," Reverend Mother said. "These are the Johnsons. They're new to our parish. Their son, Dante here, will be in your class."

"How wonderful to meet you," Maggie said. She shook hands with Dante.

"I'm Robert, and this is my wife Barbara," the man said.

She shook hands with them.

"It's so nice to meet all of you."

"I'll leave you all to get acquainted," Reverend Mother said and crossed the room to another group.

"We're so excited for Dante to start school. We've heard such good things about you," Barbara said.

"Aw. Thank you. I look forward to having him. We have fun in my class."

"You know, I used to be a nun," Barbara said.

Something weird went off inside of Maggie. At first, it was a knot in her gut and then she felt like she'd met a kindred spirit. But she hadn't left the convent, so they really didn't have anything in common.

"Really? Is that right?"

"And Robert here used to be a priest."

"No way."

"Yes," Barbara said. "We fell in love and had to leave our callings to be together, but we did. Because we couldn't not be together."

"That's so sweet." Maggie felt very uncomfortable. She had chosen her vows over love. Had she made a mistake? Then she remembered the dream, still so very vivid in her mind, and knew she'd made the right decision.

"We need to be somewhere, so we should be going, but why don't you come over for dinner tonight?" Barbara said. "I'd love to get to know you better."

"That would be great, but I don't have a car."

"Robert can pick you up. What do you say to five o'clock? That way we can have drinks before dinner."

"Sounds good to me," Maggie said.

"Great. I'll see you then," Robert said, and they left.

Maggie mingled with the few people who were left, then helped clean up. She left the hall with a sense of trepidation, worried that Alex might be waiting for her. But she wasn't so Maggie cut through the gardens and went to her room. She was working on lesson plans for the following day when Reverend Mother stopped by her room.

"What are you doing?" Reverend Mother said.

"Lesson plans. I'll admit I'll be happy when regular school starts so I can focus just on my grade level."

"I'm sure that will be easier. But you've been a Godsend this summer with the kids."

"Aw. Thank you."

"So, how was it seeing Ms. Foster today?"

"It was fine," Maggie lied. "We spoke for a few minutes, and then I mingled. No biggie."

"Oh, I'm so glad to hear that. And she didn't wait for you after the social?"

"No, ma'am. She was gone when I came out of the hall."

"That's fantastic. I guess you two just needed some time away from each other to get over things."

"Yeah. I guess we did."

"What are you doing for dinner tonight?" Mother Superior said.

"I'm having dinner with the Johnsons. Robert will be here at five to pick me up."

"That's fantastic news. I'm so glad to hear that. I think that'll do you good."

"I think so, too," Maggie said.

"Five o'clock did you say?"

"Yes, ma'am."

Reverend Mother checked her watch.

"Well, it's four thirty now. You'd better get ready."

"Oh, I had no idea. Thank you, ma'am."

"Don't stay out too late. It's a school night, after all."

"Yes, ma'am."

Reverend Mother left Maggie alone with her thoughts. How would she do at dinner knowing Barbara and Robert had thrown away their vows to be with each other? She didn't approve, but she was not put on this Earth to judge others. She would go and learn more about them, listen to their stories, and hopefully have a pleasant evening.

At five o'clock, she walked out to the parking lot. She saw Robert sitting in his car waiting for her. She climbed into the car.

"Hi, Sister Mary Margaret. I'm so glad you could make it. We're so excited to get to know you better. We like knowing the nuns who teach Dante."

"And I'm looking forward to getting to know you guys, as well. I always appreciate parents who take this kind of interest in their children's education."

"Dante is our only child, so we have the energy to invest in his education."

"That's great."

"Do you like red wine? Or would you prefer something stronger?" Robert said. "We only have wine at the house, but I'll be happy to stop and pick up something stronger if you'd like."

"Oh, thank you, but wine will be fine. I do enjoy a nice red wine."

"We have some good wines. This Central Coast is packed with good wineries."

"Yes, it is."

The conversation was light and easy, and soon they pulled up in front of a nice large modern house in the Ferrini Heights area.

"Wow. This is a nice place you have here," Maggie said.

"Thanks. We like it. It looks a lot bigger from the outside. Obviously, we don't need a lot of space for just the three of us."

They got out of the car, and Robert opened the door for Maggie. She walked in to find an entry hallway filled with Native American artwork. There were paintings and masks and statues.

"This is beautiful," she said.

Barbara came in from a side door.

"Hello, Sister. I'm so glad you could make it."

"I'm very happy to be here."

"Would you like a glass of wine before dinner?"

"That sounds wonderful. Thank you."

"We have red or white. What's your choice?" Barbara said.

"Sister Mary Margaret is a fan of reds, just like us," Robert said.

"Great. We've got some good local Cabernet. Will that do?"

"That would be great," Maggie said.

"Come in. Come in," Robert said, as he escorted Maggie into a spacious living room. It, too, was decorated in Native American furnishings. It was comfortable, and Maggie relaxed into the soft leather couch.

Barbara handed each of them a glass of wine.

"Dinner smells delicious," Maggie said.

"Thanks. It's lasagna. My great-grandma's recipe," Barbara said.

"Well, it smells divine."

"Barbara works magic in the kitchen."

Barbara smiled radiantly at Robert. Maggie wondered if she'd ever seen two people so deeply in love. Was that how she'd looked with Alex? She shook the thought from her mind.

They had another glass of wine.

"So, where do you guys work?" Maggie said.

"I'm a nurse," Barbara said. "And Robert is a professor at Cal Poly."

"Nice."

"We both are very passionate about our jobs," Robert said. "As I'm sure you are about yours."

"Oh, yes. Very," Maggie said. "I love teaching. And I'm devoted to God, so being a nun is a natural for me."

They called Dante downstairs to the table for dinner. Robert opened another bottle of wine.

"This is a Shiraz. We really like it with our lasagna."

Maggie took a sip.

"It's quite nice," she said.

Once they were all served, Maggie turned her attention to Dante.

"So, Dante," she said. "What's your favorite subject?"

"P.E."

"Dante is quite the athlete," Robert said. "He'll be playing pee-wee football when the season starts. He's very excited."

"That's great," Maggie said. "So, outside of P.E., what's your favorite subject?"

"Science."

Maggie raised her eyebrows. She wondered how smart Dante was. While they hadn't spoken much, his mannerisms indicated he was very well behaved. She wondered if that transferred to his schoolwork.

"I love science," Maggie said. "Maybe you can help me come up with some experiments to do in class."

Dante's eyes lit up.

"That would be awesome."

"Great. We'll do that once school starts."

"Thanks."

"Oh, no, Dante. Thank *you*."

They finished dinner and the wine, and Dante went upstairs to play video games, leaving the adults to chat.

"Dinner was delicious," Maggie said as Robert poured her a glass of Pinot Noir. Maggie was feeling relaxed and more than slightly buzzed by then. She sank farther into the couch.

"So, I can't stop thinking that the two of you had once taken the Holy Vows. And you fell in love. I'm a romantic at heart, but I still can't help but wonder, what made you decide to give up your vows for a relationship? I mean, how did you know it was the right thing to do?"

"Oh, we prayed hard over the decision. Both on our own and together. And it just seemed that God wanted us to be happy. And we were no longer happy with our vows. So we became lay people. We stayed in the Church though, as we believe in the teachings of Catholicism."

Maggie sipped her wine and felt more mellow than she had in a long time. Unfortunately, the wine seemed to loosen her lips.

"I had an affair once," she heard herself say.

Barbara crossed over and sat next to her on the sofa. She took her hands in her own.

"Oh, honey. It happens. Why didn't you leave the sisterhood? Were you happy in your relationship?"

"I was. I was so happy. But I couldn't leave the convent. I loved it, too."

Maggie told herself she'd said too much. She'd be teaching these people's kid, for crying out loud.

"But, Sister, love is an important part of our life. God gave us the ability to love. When we find true love, we can't walk away."

"Well, as I said, I love the convent, too." Maggie hoped that would be the last on the conversation.

"May I ask why, if you loved them both, you chose the convent?"

"I had a dream. And in it, God told me to serve Him."

She told them about the dream she'd had. She felt the tears pool in her eyes. She tried to blink them away, but one slipped down her cheek.

"Oh, honey," Barbara said as she squeezed her hands. "It's clear you still have feelings for this man."

"It was a woman," Maggie said softly.

"Oh wow. So a double whammy for you," Robert said. "That had to be tough."

"It was."

"So you had this dream," Robert said. "Has God ever spoken to you in a dream before?"

"Never. It was a first. But I'd been praying for guidance for so long. I'd prayed to Him for help to decide which way to go. And that dream told me the answer."

"You know dreams are just manifestations of our subconscious, don't you?" Robert said.

"I know this. But it was God, and He was speaking to me. I know it."

"But, Sister, God doesn't speak through your mind. He speaks through your heart. God is love," Barbara said.

Maggie sat silently for a minute. Had she made the wrong decision after all? No, she was sure God had wanted her to stay in the convent. But what the Johnsons were saying made so much sense. Should she have listened to her heart and stayed with Alex? She was confused.

"Well," she finally said. "I made up my mind, so now I'll stick with it."

"I hope you'll do some real soul searching after our talk, though. I mean, I'd love to have you teach Dante. I have heard wonderful things about you. But if you're doing it at the expense of true love, well, I just don't think that's right," Barbara said.

"You know, I've had a lovely time tonight, but it's getting late and I have to teach summer school in the morning."

"Oh, I'm sorry," Barbara said. "I hope we didn't upset you."

"Not at all. I enjoyed myself. And you gave me plenty to think about."

"Thinking isn't always a bad thing," Robert said. "But come on. I'll take you home."

They drove home in easy conversation until they arrived at the convent.

"Thank you again for a wonderful evening," Maggie said.

"Thank you for coming over. And, Sister? Please give some thought to what we talked about. We'd love to see you happy."

"Thanks. And I will."

Maggie had a hard time walking a straight line into the convent. She got to her room and stripped, then poured herself into bed.

Chapter Twenty-three

Maggie woke the next morning with a headache and an upset stomach. She no more wanted to teach than to climb Mount Everest. But she knew she had to. She'd had far too much wine the night before, so she had no one to blame but herself. She took a long shower, then went to the dining room. She made herself a waffle, hoping it would absorb any alcohol still left in her system. She picked up a bag lunch and went to school.

She made it through the day and decided to grade papers in her room rather than in the classroom. She walked back to the convent and bumped into Reverend Mother.

"Hello, my child," Reverend Mother said.

"Hello. Why aren't you in your office?"

"I was coming to your room to see if you were home. Walk with me to my office?"

"Of course."

They got to her office.

"What can I do for you?" Maggie said.

"I was wondering how dinner went last night. But first, do you feel okay? You don't look too good."

"I'm fine. And dinner was nice."

"I didn't see you before curfew."

"I made it home right at ten," Maggie said.

"Good. Did you have a chance to visit with their son?"

"Yes. Dante and I talked at dinner."

"Good. He seems like such a nice young man."

"He really does."

"And his parents? Did you get along with them?" Mother Superior said.

"I did." Her stomach was in knots. She had so much to think about. Did she dare broach any of it to Reverend Mother? She decided to at least tell part of it. "Did you know he used to be a priest and she used to be a nun?"

Reverend Mother sat silently for a moment.

"I didn't know that."

"Yeah. They were quite interesting."

"I hope you didn't get any wild ideas after spending the evening with them?"

"I don't know, Reverend Mother. I'm kind of back to being torn." The words were out before she could stop them.

"What do you need to do to prove to yourself you made the right decision?"

"I'm not sure. I think maybe I need to see Alex."

"You do, do you?" Reverend Mother said.

"Yes, ma'am. Just to prove to myself I'm over her. I thought I'd see if she was free for dinner Friday night. I'd rather see her sooner, but I think it would be best to wait."

"I'm not sure you're making a good decision in seeing her."

"I have to know, Reverend Mother. I have to know I made the right decision in staying with the convent."

"I know you do. But I don't want you seeing Ms. Foster. I think it's dangerous."

"It's only dangerous if my heart tells me she's where I need to stay," Maggie said.

"And I don't know if I'm willing to take that chance."

"Reverend Mother. Would you have me living in the convent never knowing? Always doubting?"

"No. I wouldn't like that at all."

"Then let me spend Friday evening with Alex. That way, whatever answer we come up with, we'll know is the right one."

"And if you remain torn," Reverend Mother said, "I suppose then you'll have to keep seeing her until your mind is made up?"

"I won't be torn. If I'm still in love with her, I follow my heart. If not, I stay with the Church. Besides, Reverend Mother, we haven't considered her feelings yet. She might not want to see me again."

Reverend Mother harrumphed.

"That'll be the day. Maggie, you know you're loved and respected here. But I just don't know if you're strong enough to withstand her pull. After all, you weren't before."

"I didn't want to be before. I told you that. I was already attracted to her," Maggie said. "But now I'm dedicated to the Church, so she's got so much more to overcome."

Even as she said it, she knew she was lying. The sight of Alex the day before had driven her crazy. She just wanted to know if Alex was still in love with her. If so, they could start a life together, if Alex would go for that.

"I can see your mind's made up, my child. I fear I'm sending you into the lion's den, but so be it. Have dinner on Friday night. And may God be with you."

"Thank you."

Maggie went back to her room and sat at her desk. She pulled out the faded paper with Alex's number on it. She walked down the hall to the phone and called her.

"Hello?"

The sound of Alex's voice made Maggie's heart skip a beat.

"Alex?" she said.

"Yes. Maggie? Is everything okay?"

"Oh, yes. Don't worry. Everything is fine. I just had a favor to ask of you."

Maggie heard her voice shake. She tried to keep calm, but she was a nervous wreck.

"You don't sound okay, but if you say so. So, what's the favor? Anything. If I can do it, I will."

"Will you take me to dinner Friday night?"

"Friday night? What's the occasion? Aren't you supposed to eat at the convent?" Alex said.

"I got permission to miss dinner Friday night. And I'd like to see you."

"Are you sure everything's okay? I'm not sure I understand."

"There's nothing to understand," Maggie said. "I just thought it would be nice to have dinner together."

"Okay. All right then. I can do that. What time should I pick you up?"

"That's up to you."

"I'll pick you up at three. Right after work. Then we can hang out by the pool for a few before we go to dinner. Sound good?"

"Sounds good," Maggie said.

"I'll see you then."

Maggie hung up the phone and wanted to skip down the hall to her room. She was going to see Alex on Friday. And it would be away from the prying eyes of Reverend Mother. Oh, yes, Maggie was excited.

When six o'clock rolled around, Maggie was in the dining room waiting for Reverend Mother to say grace. When she'd finished, Maggie dug into her dinner, her appetite back with a vengeance. Reverend Mother walked over and sat next to her. So much for Maggie's appetite. She set her utensils down.

"Did you make your phone call?" Reverend Mother said.

"I did."

"And?"

"And she's picking me up at three."

"Three?" Reverend Mother said. "That's awfully early."

"We'll swim before dinner."

"Did you tell her why you called her?"

"No, ma'am. I just told her I wanted to have dinner with her," Maggie said.

"And what was her response?"

"Surprise. Concern. But mostly, surprise."

"Yes. I'm sure she was surprised to hear from you after all this time. I just hope you can be strong, Maggie."

"It's not a matter of being strong. It's a matter of finding out where my heart truly lies."

"Yes. I suppose it is. Well, good luck."

She left and Maggie finished her dinner.

The rest of the week went smoothly for Maggie. She had no more talking-tos from Reverend Mother. Her classes were well behaved, regardless of the fact that there was only one more week until summer school ended. Finally, Friday afternoon rolled around. Maggie finished her classes, took her paperwork back to her room, grabbed her swimsuit, and walked out to the parking lot at just after three.

Alex was waiting in her truck.

"Sorry I'm late," Maggie said.

"Oh, no worries. I'm just happy to see you. I'm still not sure I understand why you wanted to see me. And why Mother Superior would approve it, but I'm glad it's happening."

"So, where are we going for dinner?"

"I thought we'd try the Creekside Brewing Company. It should be fun. And it's nice and casual."

"Sounds good to me."

"It's more about the beer there than the wine, but they have wine there, too, I'm sure."

"Excellent. Though I might have beer. I had too much wine Sunday night."

"Really?" Alex laughed. "What did you do Sunday night?"

"I had dinner with some new parishioners. And the wine was flowing all night."

"Good for you. I'm glad you had a good time."

"I guess I did."

Alex glanced over at Maggie.

"You guess you did?" she said.

"It was harsh in some ways."

"How so?"

"We can talk about it at your place."

"Okay."

They pulled into Alex's driveway and got out of the truck. Once inside the house, Maggie wanted to throw herself at Alex. She wanted to tell her she loved her, she'd always loved her, and she needed to feel her arms around her. She missed the kisses they'd shared so many times as soon as that door had closed. She slid her hands into her pockets to keep from touching Alex.

"So, um, you want to hit the pool?" Alex said.

"Sure."

"I'll go upstairs and change. You can use the guest room downstairs."

"Okay. Thanks."

Maggie changed into her suit. It felt so odd to wear a suit with Alex. She longed to be naked with her, to feel the water and Alex on her and in her. She knew she loved Alex, and, if given the chance, she'd go back to her in a heartbeat. It would mean leaving the convent, but if God truly wanted her to be happy, He would want her to be with Alex.

Alex knocked on the door.

"Are you ready?" Alex said.

"Yeah. I'm coming."

Maggie stepped out into the hallway and saw Alex in her board shorts and tank top. She looked amazing. She followed her out to the patio.

"Want to swim some laps?" Alex said.

"Sure."

They swam for a while, then Maggie took her usual spot on the steps. She watched Alex cut through the water. Her mouth drooled over the sight of her muscular form. When Alex swam over to her, she scooted over on the step to make room for her.

Alex sat.

"You ready to talk yet?"

"I don't know. I think I am, but then maybe not. Maybe I should wait until dinner."

"Suit yourself," Alex said. "I'm just happy to have this time with you."

"Yeah. It's nice."

"Almost just like old times."

"Almost," Maggie said.

They dried off in the sun, then went inside to get dressed for dinner. Once at the restaurant, Alex showed her impatience.

"Okay. We're here. Now, what's going on?"

Maggie wrung her hands. Her eyes filled with tears. This was the moment of truth, but it had to happen. If Alex didn't love her or want to pursue a relationship with her, then it would hurt, but she could go back to the convent knowing it was where she belonged.

"Mags? Why are you crying?"

Frustrated, Maggie wiped away a tear.

"What's wrong? How can I help?" Alex said.

Maggie took a deep breath.

"Alex, did you love me?" she said.

"Oh, Maggie. You know I did."

"Do you still?"

"I can't answer that question. If I allow myself to still love you it hurts too much."

"So, you're over me."

"I can't say that, either," Alex said. "Where is all this going? If you're only trying to open old scabs, I'm not really interested."

"No. It's nothing like that. Honest."

"Okay, so what's this about?"

"You know when I told you I had too much wine Sunday night?" Maggie said.

"Yeah. Were you on a date?"

"Oh, no. Nothing like that. I was with a family. A mom and dad whose son will be in my class next year."

"Okay. Sounds innocent enough. I'm still listening." Alex said.

"Well, the couple, the mom and dad? They used to be in the Church. He was a priest, and she was a nun. They met and fell in love."

"Oh, wow."

"Yeah." Maggie waited until what she'd said sank in.

"So, that affects us how?"

"So, we talked about us and my dream and my staying with the convent."

"Yeah?" Alex said. "And what did they say about the dream?"

"That God doesn't speak to us through our minds. He speaks to us through our hearts. That God is love."

"That makes sense."

They stopped speaking while their food was served. They each took a bite, then looked at each other. Maggie took another deep breath.

"Well, it made me wonder. I mean, I love you. I always have. And I wonder if maybe I made the wrong decision."

Alex sat back in her chair. She let out a heavy sigh.

"I don't know what to say, Maggie."

They ate in silence for a few minutes. Maggie took a sip of her beer.

"Say something."

"What are you asking me? Are you asking me to make the decision for you?"

"No. Well, yeah, I guess. I don't know. I just need to know how you feel about me. Because if you still love me and I still love you and you're willing to try to make it work, I'm saying I'd be willing to leave the convent for you."

Alex downed her beer.

"That's a lot of pressure on me," she said.

"And it's fine if you don't still love me. Or if you're not willing to settle down. Then I'll know the convent is the place for me."

"I don't know what to say, Maggie. It's up to me whether or not you give up your calling. Your sacred vows. It just doesn't feel right that I make that decision for you," Alex said.

"No. I'll be the one making the decision. And I'll own the decision. But if there is no us, I'll be happy to spend the rest of my days at the convent."

"Shit, Maggie. You know I love you. I've never stopped loving you."

"Yeah?" Maggie's eyes filled with tears of joy.

"Yeah."

"And are you willing to let me move in? To have a real relationship with me?"

"I'd like nothing more."

"Oh, Alex."

Alex went to Maggie's side of the table and pulled her into a tight hug.

"Are you still eating?" Alex said.

"No."

Alex signaled for the check. She paid and they hurried to her truck. Once back at the house, Alex couldn't keep her hands off Maggie. She pressed against her and kissed her hard. The feel of Alex's mouth on hers was familiar and welcome, and oh so erotic. Maggie kissed her back with the need that threatened to consume her. Suddenly, Alex backed up.

"Should we wait? I mean, should we hold off until you let your mother superior know your decision?"

"My decision is made, Alex. I'm going to step away from the Church, so as far as I'm concerned, my vows no longer apply. Sure, I'll talk to Reverend Mother tomorrow and we'll start the process to relieve me of them, but for the moment, I need you. I've waited far too long."

They made their way upstairs to Alex's bedroom. Alex slowly and deliberately undressed Maggie. She kissed every spot of skin as she exposed it.

"You feel amazing," Maggie said. She lay on the bed and watched as Alex climbed out of her own clothes.

They kissed, a hard, passionate kiss that conveyed their desire for each other. When Maggie felt Alex's tongue enter her mouth, she felt herself grow wet. She rolled over on top of Alex and felt Alex's hands move up and down her body. They stopped to cup her butt and Maggie thought she'd go mad with desire.

Alex rolled over so she was on top. She didn't stay there long. She climbed off her and skimmed her hand down her body. She bent her head to take one of Maggie's breasts in her mouth. She ran her hand lower until it came to where her legs met. Alex slipped her fingers inside her and stroked her deep. Maggie moaned as the feelings Alex was creating filled her.

Alex moved lower until she could take Maggie's clit in her mouth. She continued to move her fingers in and out as she sucked her slick clit.

"Oh, my God," Maggie said. "Oh, yes. Oh, dear God, yes." She felt the energy form deep inside her. She held it in as long as she could and then let loose as the orgasms racked her body.

"I've missed you so much, Maggie," Alex said.

"I've missed you, too."

Maggie kissed Alex and savored her own flavor on her lips. She placed her hand on Alex's breast and pinched her nipple. Alex moaned in appreciation. Maggie slipped her hand lower and found Alex wet and warm and ready for her.

"You feel so amazing," Maggie said.

"So do you. Take me, Maggie."

"I will."

Maggie thrust her fingers as deep as she could go. She ran her fingertips over all the soft spots she found in there. She remembered Alex's favorite spot and rubbed it until Alex screamed as she came.

After, they lay together for a few minutes before Maggie spoke.

"I hate to do this, but I need to get home by curfew."

Alex kissed her.

"I know. I realize this. Soon, we won't have to do this anymore. You'll be able to spend the night with me."

"I anticipate that starting tomorrow."

"Call me and let me know how everything goes."

"I will," Maggie said.

They got dressed and climbed into Alex's truck. Alex took Maggie's hand.

"I love you," she said.

"I love you, too."

And Alex dropped Maggie off at the convent for the last time ever.

About the Author

MJ Williamz was raised on California's central coast, which she left at age seventeen to pursue an education. She graduated from Chico State, and it was in Chico that she rediscovered her love of writing. It wasn't until she moved to Portland, however, that her writing really took off, with the publication of her first short story in 2003.

MJ is the author of sixteen books, including three Goldie Award winners. She has also had over thirty short stories published, most of them erotica with a few romances and a few horrors thrown in for good measure. She lives in Houston with her wife, fellow author Laydin Michaels, and their fur babies. You can reach her at mjwilliamz@aol.com.

Books Available from Bold Strokes Books

Against All Odds by Kris Bryant, Maggie Cummings, M. Ullrich. Peyton and Tory escaped death once, but will they survive when Bradley's determined to make his kill rate one hundred percent? (978-1-163555-193-8)

Autumn's Light by Aurora Rey. Casual hookups aren' t supposed to include romantic dinners and meeting the family. Can Mat Pero see beyond the heartbreak that led her to keep her worlds so separate, and will Graham Connor be waiting if she does? (978-1-163555-272-0)

Breaking the Rules by Larkin Rose. When Virginia and Carmen are thrown together by an embarrassing mistake they find out their stubborn determination isn't so heroic after all. (978-1-163555-261-4)

Broad Awakening by Mickey Brent. In the sequel to *Underwater Vibes*, Hélène and Sylvie find ruts in their road to eternal bliss. (978-1-163555-270-6)

Broken Vows by MJ Williamz. Sister Mary Margaret must reconcile her divided heart or risk losing a love that just might be heaven sent. (978-1-163555-022-1)

Flesh and Gold by Ann Aptaker. Havana, 1952, where art thief and smuggler Cantor Gold dodges gangland bullets and mobsters' schemes while she searches Havana' s steamy Red Light district for her kidnapped love. (978-1-163555-153-2)

Isle of Broken Years by Jane Fletcher. Spanish noblewoman Catalina de Valasco is in peril, even before the pirates holding her for ransom sail into seas destined to become known as the Bermuda Triangle. (978-1-163555-175-4)

Love Like This by Melissa Brayden. Hadley Cooper and Spencer Adair set out to take the fashion world by storm. If only they knew their hearts were about to be taken. (978-1-163555-018-4)

Secrets On the Clock by Nicole Disney. Jenna and Danielle love their jobs helping endangered children, but that might not be enough to stop them from breaking the rules by falling in love. (978-1-163555-292-8)

Unexpected Partners by Michelle Larkin. Dr. Chloe Maddox tries desperately to deny her attraction for Detective Dana Blake as they flee from a serial killer who's hunting them both. (978-1-163555-203-4)

A Fighting Chance by T. L. Hayes. Will Lou be able to come to terms with her past to give love a fighting chance? (978-1-163555-257-7)

Chosen by Brey Willows. When the choice is adapt or die, can love save us all? (978-1-163555-110-5)

Death Checks In by David S. Pederson. Despite Heath's promises to Alan to not get involved, Heath can't resist investigating a shopkeeper's murder in Chicago, which dashes their plans for a romantic weekend getaway. (978-1-163555-329-1)

Gnarled Hollow by Charlotte Greene. After they are invited to study a secluded nineteenth-century estate, a former English professor and a group of historians discover that they will have to fight against the unknown if they have any hope of staying alive. (978-1-163555-235-5)

Jacob's Grace by C.P. Rowlands. Captain Tag Becket wants to keep her head down and her past behind her, but her feelings for AJ's second-in-command, Grace Fields, makes keeping secrets next to impossible. (978-1-163555-187-7)

On the Fly by PJ Trebelhorn. Hockey player Courtney Abbott is content with her solitary life until visiting concert violinist Lana Caruso makes her second-guess everything she always thought she wanted. (978-1-163555-255-3)

Passionate Rivals by Radclyffe. Professional rivalry and long-simmering passions create a combustible combination when Emmett McCabe and Sydney Stevens are forced to work together, especially when past attractions won't stay buried. (978-1-163555-231-7)

Proxima Five by Missouri Vaun. When geologist Leah Warren crash-lands on a preindustrial planet and is claimed by its tyrant, Tiago, will clan warrior Keegan's love for Leah give her the strength to defeat him? (978-1-163555-122-8)

Racing Hearts by Dena Blake. When you cross a hot-tempered race car mechanic with a reckless cop, the result can only be spontaneous combustion. (978-1-163555-251-5)

Shadowboxer by Jessica L. Webb. Jordan McAddie is prepared to keep her street kids safe from a dangerous underground protest group, but she isn't prepared for her first love to walk back into her life. (978-1-163555-267-6)

The Tattered Lands by Barbara Ann Wright. As Vandra and Lilani strive to make peace, they slowly fall in love. With mistrust and murder surrounding them, only their faith in each other can keep their plan to save the world from falling apart. (978-1-163555-108-2)

Captive by Donna K. Ford. To escape a human trafficking ring, Greyson Cooper and Olivia Danner become players in a game of deceit and violence. Will their love stand a chance? (978-1-63555-215-7)

Crossing the Line by CF Frizzell. The Mob discovers a nemesis within its ranks, and in the ultimate retaliation, draws Stick McLaughlin from anonymity by threatening everything she holds dear. (978-1-63555-161-7)

Love's Verdict by Carsen Taite. Attorneys Landon Holt and Carly Pachett want the exact same thing: the only open partnership spot at their prestigious criminal defense firm. But will they compromise their careers for love? (978-1-63555-042-9)

Precipice of Doubt by Mardi Alexander & Laurie Eichler. Can Cole Jameson resist her attraction to her boss, veterinarian Jodi Bowman, or will she risk a workplace romance and her heart? (978-1-63555-128-0)

Savage Horizons by CJ Birch. Captain Jordan Kellow's feelings for Lt. Ali Ash have her past and future colliding, setting in motion a series of events that strands her crew in an unknown galaxy thousands of light years from home. (978-1-63555-250-8)

Secrets of the Last Castle by A. Rose Mathieu. When Elizabeth Campbell represents a young man accused of murdering an elderly woman, her investigation leads to an abandoned plantation that reveals many dark Southern secrets. (978-1-63555-240-9)

Take Your Time by VK Powell. A neurotic parrot brings police officer Grace Booker and temporary veterinarian Dr. Dani Wingate together in the tiny town of Pine Cone, but their unexpected attraction keeps the sparks flying. (978-1-63555-130-3)

The Last Seduction by Ronica Black. When you allow true love to elude you once and you desperately regret it, are you brave enough to grab it when it comes around again? (978-1-63555-211-9)

The Shape of You by Georgia Beers. Rebecca McCall doesn't play it safe, but when sexy Spencer Thompson joins her workout class, their non-stop sparring forces her to face her ultimate challenge—a chance at love. (978-1-63555-217-1)

Exposed by MJ Williamz. The closet is no place to live if you want to find true love. (978-1-62639-989-1)

Force of Fire: Toujours a Vous by Ali Vali. Immortals Kendal and Piper welcome their new child and celebrate the defeat of an old enemy, but another ancient evil is about to awaken deep in the jungles of Costa Rica. (978-1-63555-047-4)

Holding Their Place by Kelly A. Wacker. Together Dr. Helen Connery and ambulance driver Julia March, discover that goodness, love, and passion can be found in the most unlikely and even dangerous places during WWI. (978-1-63555-338-3)

Landing Zone by Erin Dutton. Can a career veteran finally discover a love stronger than even her pride? (978-1-63555-199-0)

Love at Last Call by M. Ullrich. Is balancing business, friendship, and love more than any willing woman can handle? (978-1-63555-197-6)

Pleasure Cruise by Yolanda Wallace. Spencer Collins and Amy Donovan have few things in common, but a Caribbean cruise offers both women an unexpected chance to face one of their greatest fears: falling in love. (978-1-63555-219-5)

Running Off Radar by MB Austin. Maji's plans to win Rose back are interrupted when work intrudes and duty calls her to help a SEAL team stop a Russian mobster from harvesting gold from the bottom of Sitka Sound. (978-1-63555-152-5)

Shadow of the Phoenix by Rebecca Harwell. In the final battle for the fate of Storm's Quarry, even Nadya's and Shay's powers may not be enough. (978-1-63555-181-5)

Take a Chance by D. Jackson Leigh. There's hardly a woman within fifty miles of Pine Cone that veterinarian Trip Beaumont can't charm, except for the irritating new cop, Jamie Grant, who keeps leaving parking tickets on her truck. (978-1-63555-118-1)

The Outcasts by Alexa Black. Spacebus driver Sue Jones is running from her past. When she crash-lands on a faraway world, the Outcast Kara might be her chance for redemption. (978-1-63555-242-3)

Alias by Cari Hunter. A car crash leaves a woman with no memory and no identity. Together with Detective Bronwen Pryce, she fights to uncover a truth that might just kill them both. (978-1-63555-221-8)

Death in Time by Robyn Nyx. Working in the past is hell on your future. (978-1-63555-053-5)

Hers to Protect by Nicole Disney. High school sweethearts Kaia and Adrienne will have to see past their differences and survive the vengeance of a brutal gang if they want to be together. (978-1-63555-229-4)

Of Echoes Born by 'Nathan Burgoine. A collection of queer fantasy short stories set in Canada from Lambda Literary Award finalist 'Nathan Burgoine. (978-1-63555-096-2)

Perfect Little Worlds by Clifford Mae Henderson. Lucy can't hold the secret any longer. Twenty-six years ago, her sister did the unthinkable. (978-1-63555-164-8)

Room Service by Fiona Riley. Interior designer Olivia likes stability, but when work brings footloose Savannah into her world and into a new city every month, Olivia must decide if what makes her comfortable is what makes her happy. (978-1-63555-120-4)

Sparks Like Ours by Melissa Brayden. Professional surfers Gia Malone and Elle Britton can't deny their chemistry on and off the beach. But only one can win… (978-1-63555-016-0)

Take My Hand by Missouri Vaun. River Hemsworth arrives in Georgia intent on escaping quickly, but when she crashes her Mercedes into the Clip 'n Curl, sexy Clay Cahill ends up rescuing more than her car. (978-1-63555-104-4)

The Last Time I Saw Her by Kathleen Knowles. Lane Hudson only has twelve days to win back Alison's heart. That is if she can gather the courage to try. (978-1-63555-067-2)

Wayworn Lovers by Gun Brooke. Will agoraphobic composer Giselle Bonnaire and Tierney Edwards, a wandering soul who can't remain in one place for long, trust in the passionate love destiny hands them? (978-1-62639-995-2)

Lightning Source UK Ltd.
Milton Keynes UK
UKHW04f1446251018
331198UK00001B/92/P